"I'm not going to enjoy beating you, Cord."

Raising her eyes to his, she offered an apologetic smile. "I do hope you come in second."

Cord laughed, loving her innocent sincerity. "Honey, I'm riding to win," he vowed, catching her chin in his hand. "But when I do, you remember how much work you've put into that bull-headed cayuse of mine. You'll be a winner, too."

"I'll take his award for being best conditioned, thank you."

"I'll take his trainer—" Stretching out beside her, Cord reached over her hip and filled his hand with the target it had been itching for all evening. She lifted her head for the kiss she knew was coming. She returned it, and he groaned, then whispered into her mouth, "—thank you."

MEN at WORK

1. HOODWINKED—
   Diana Palmer
2. MACKENZIE'S LADY—
   Dallas Schulze
3. AN IRRITATING MAN—
   Lass Small
4. WINDSTORM—
   Connie Bennett
5. HEAVEN SHARED—
   Cathy Gillen Thacker
6. CONFIDENTIALLY YOURS—
   Helen R. Myers
7. BODY AND SOUL—
   Janice Kaiser
8. DESTINATIONS SOUTH—
   Elizabeth Bevarly
9. DEFYING GRAVITY—
   Rachel Lee
10. UNDERCOVER—
    Jasmine Cresswell
11. GLASS HOUSES—
    Anne Stuart
12. NIGHT OF THE HUNTER—
    Jennifer Greene
13. A REBEL AT HEART—
    Gina Wilkins
14. MISS LIZ'S PASSION—
    Sherryl Woods
15. MAGIC AND MOONBEAMS—
    Margot Dalton
16. HANDSOME DEVIL—
    Joan Hohl
17. ANGEL VS. MacLEAN—
    Cait London
18. HEALING SYMPATHY—
    Gina Wilkins
19. SOUND OF SUMMER—
    Annette Broadrick
20. THE FOREVER ROSE—
    Curtiss Ann Matlock
21. KNIGHT SPARKS—
    Mary Lynn Baxter
22. FIT TO BE TIED—
    Joan Johnston
23. A SEASON FOR BUTTERFLIES—
    Laurie Paige
24. CAPTIVE OF FATE—
    Lindsay McKenna
25. UNDER THE COVERS—
    Roseanne Williams

26. STARK LIGHTNING—
    Elaine Barbieri
27. THE PRINCE & THE SHOWGIRL—
    JoAnn Ross
28. MORE THAN FRIENDS—
    Susan Mallery
29. WE GIVE THANKS—
    Linda Randall Wisdom
30. COULD IT BE MAGIC—
    Gina Wilkins
31. EXPIRATION DATE—
    Aimée Thurlo
32. IT'S ONLY TEMPORARY—
    Cathy Gillen Thacker
33. A CLASSIC ENCOUNTER—
    Emilie Richards
34. THE MIGHTY QUINN—
    Candace Schuler
35. SILVER NOOSE—
    Patricia Gardner Evans
36. THE MIRACLE—
    Muriel Jensen
37. A FRAGILE BEAUTY—
    Lucy Gordon
38. FEAR FAMILIAR—
    Caroline Burnes
39. SOMETHING WORTH KEEPING—
    Kathleen Eagle
40. DILLON AFTER DARK—
    Leandra Logan
41. THE HEART CLUB—
    Margaret St. George
42. ONLY IN THE MOONLIGHT—
    Vicki Lewis Thompson
43. TO DIE FOR—
    M.J. Rodgers
44. THE COWBOY'S MISTRESS—
    Cathy Gillen Thacker
45. ALL MY TOMORROWS—
    Karen Young
46. PLAYING FOR TIME—
    Barbara Bretton
47. THE PERFECT MATCH—
    Ginna Gray
48. HOTSHOT—
    Kathleen Korbel
49. VALENTINE'S KNIGHT—
    Renee Roszel
50. STORMWALKER—
    Bronwyn Williams

—MILLIONAIRE'S CLUB   —BOARDROOM BOYS   —MAGNIFICENT MEN

—TALL, DARK & SMART   —DOCTOR, DOCTOR   —MEN OF THE WEST

—MEN OF STEEL   —MEN IN UNIFORM

MEN at WORK

KATHLEEN EAGLE

SOMETHING WORTH KEEPING

MEN of STEEL

Silhouette Books

Published by Silhouette Books

America's Publisher of Contemporary Romance

SILHOUETTE BOOKS
300 East 42nd St.,
New York, N. Y. 10017

ISBN 0-373-81051-2

SOMETHING WORTH KEEPING

Copyright © 1987 by Kathleen Eagle

This edition published by arrangement with Harlequin Books S.A.

® and TM are trademarks of Harlequin Books S.A., used under license.
Trademarks indicated with ® are registered in the United States Patent
and Trademark Office, the Canadian Trade Marks Office and in other
countries.

Printed in U.S.A.

Dear Reader,

MEN AT WORK. How romantic! Seriously, is there anything more appealing to a woman than a man with a tool belt? Red toolboxes are good, too, as long as they come with a man who knows how to fix things. They say a woman looks for a mate who reminds her of her father, and one of the things on my subconscious checklist must have been: Knows what to do when something breaks—including my heart!

I can tell you from experience that there's no better handyman than a cowboy, the original jack-of-all-trades. Like my husband, Clyde, farrier Cord O'Brien is the consummate cowboy. He wields his hammer over an anvil, works his magic on tame horses' hooves and wild horses' hearts. Who better to hold the heart of a privileged but lonely woman in the palm of his callused, gentle hand? This is the story of two people from very different worlds who come together to train a mustang called Freedom for a race they both intend to enter. And they both fully intend to win.

May you hear the music in your heart!

Kathleen Eagle

Please address questions and book requests to:
Silhouette Reader Service
U.S.: 3010 Walden Ave., P.O. Box 1325, Buffalo, NY 14269
Canadian: P.O. Box 609, Fort Erie, Ont. L2A 5X3

thought that come spring he would shave—give himself a chance to see what he looked like. He hadn't looked in a mirror since Christmas, and it was—what? February? The date didn't mean much up here, only the season. He lowered the brim of his black Stetson against the sun's glare and flexed broad shoulders against the snug fit of his sheepskin jacket as he considered the horse. Freedom.

If he had any choice in the matter, he would let this horse run free. After a week's tracking, O'Brien had nearly worn himself out, to say nothing of his own mountain-bred saddle horses. He'd left his base camp and his four-wheel-drive pickup behind, and all the gear he had was what he carried on his pack horse. He'd followed the band of nomads across the state line into Utah and back into Wyoming again. The roan was a survivor, but so was he. They would make a good team, O'Brien thought.

Uncoiling his long body, he reminded himself that he had no choice but to pursue the mustang until he caught him. He was a man who seldom saw anything he coveted on the other side of another man's fence, but he had to have this horse. *This* horse. He had only seven mares left, and he wanted them bred this spring. This was the only stud who could do the job. The wily horse with the mousy, *grullo*-colored roan coat had eluded him several times over the past months, and O'Brien had enjoyed the game, but time was running out for both of them.

This time the chase would be short and sweet—straight into the box canyon he'd scouted out. From there it would be downhill all the way. At the foot of that hill stood O'Brien's ranch, where he kept the remnants of a small, carefully bred herd of Spanish mustangs. Like the roan, O'Brien's mares were a vestige of the past, and this stud was a glimmer of hope for the future of the breed.

After taking the opportunity to forage for a few nibbles

of winter-brown grass during the welcome respite from the chase, the black saddle horse lifted her head as O'Brien flipped the reins back over her ears. She stood quietly to let him swing one long leg over her back and settle into the saddle.

"This is it, girl," O'Brien told her. "We've got him now. By June he'll be eating out of my hand, and by August he'll be ready to show ol' Hank Sinclair what endurance is all about." Laying the leather rein against the side of the black's neck, he clucked to her, nudged her into a pivot and shifted his weight for the ride down the hill.

Brenna Sinclair gripped the steering wheel of her rented car tightly in both hands and craned her neck, trying to see over the next rise. The road had seemed incredibly long and desolate, and she asked herself again what motive she had for coming out here. And again she had an answer for herself: the property was part of her inheritance. She owned the house her father lived in. She had never seen it, and she knew she would not be welcome there, but it was hers, and she had come to the western part of South Dakota to claim it.

Desolate as it was, the countryside was pretty, she admitted to herself. But, then, what part of the country wasn't pretty in May? By June she would be back home, and by August her South Dakota affairs would be settled, one way or another. She doubted these hills would be so pretty once they'd been browned by August's heat.

According to the map and the directions she'd been given, she was driving past land that was now hers. Grazing horses dotted the pasture on the green hill that sloped away from the two-lane highway. A sleek white mare and her dun foal stood close to the wire fence, and Brenna slowed to a stop and studied the pair. She'd had little experience with Arabians, but she'd heard they could be high-strung. The little stud colt pricked his ears in Brenna's direction, his black eyes round, his neck slightly bowed, as was characteristic of his breed. The mare lifted her head only momentarily before dismissing Brenna and returning her attention to her patch of grass.

She wouldn't mind trying a horse like this for cross-country trail riding, Brenna decided. The breed didn't have the long legs of a thoroughbred, or the stout chest of a Morgan. A quarter horse had better hindquarters. But this looked like an animal that would challenge a mountain after crossing the desert. The mare's bearing was regal. Henry Sinclair was undoubtedly as irresponsible and as crass as Brenna's mother had repeatedly said he was, but apparently he knew good horseflesh.

Slowing to negotiate the turn from paved road to gravel, Brenna eyed the towering post-and-lintel gateway and the sign stretched overhead: Pheasant Run. Home of the Sinclair Arabian. Home of Henry Sinclair, a man his daughter knew only from the photographs she'd seen in horse journals. But Henry Sinclair did not own his home. His wife had owned it, and now it belonged to Brenna.

The gravel driveway, flanked by a split-rail fence, ran a mile and a half from the highway, and the house emerged gradually from its setting as Brenna got closer.

It was a man's house. Brenna couldn't imagine her mother ever living there, not even during the three years her parents were actually supposed to have lived together. A sprawling two-story ranch house made of the lodgepole pine that grew so abundantly in this part of the country, it blended quietly with the green pines and the tan and green hills.

Other buildings became distinguishable as she approached. Corrals, barns, everything was built of wood, treated and stained a natural brown. The style was Western, right down to the mailbox with the spur-shaped handle. How her mother must have hated it.

As she parked the small car next to a red pickup with a white topper, Brenna surveyed the railed porch. Somewhere behind the house a dog was barking furiously, and someone in one of the other buildings had a band saw running. But no one came to the door. Apparently no one had heard her drive up. No one knew she was coming, and, of course, no one would welcome her.

But she had no wish to be welcome. She was here on business. The property was hers. She hadn't decided what to do with it yet—whether to kick the whole lot of them out and sell the place before heading back to Greenwich, or whether to hold on to it for a while. Henry Sinclair would never have enough money to buy it from her. If he had, surely he would have bought it long ago. She simply wanted them to know who the owner was—who held the deed to Pheasant Run.

The front door opened when Brenna mounted the plank steps to the porch. The screen door creaked as the woman came out from behind it, letting it close behind her with a dull wooden thud. A tall woman—though most people looked tall to Brenna—she wore jeans and a plaid shirt, and her ash-blond hair was pulled back in a low ponytail. She was attractive in a sturdy, substantial sense. Her puzzled frown became a tentative smile, her blue eyes friendly enough.

"You look like you might be lost," the woman said. "Did you miss the turn to Rapid City? A lot of folks do that."

"I'm not lost," Brenna informed her, inclining her chin slightly as she always did when she sought to establish herself. "I'm looking for Pheasant Run and Henry Sinclair."

"Well, you found Pheasant Run. Hen—Hank's around here somewhere. Come on in." The woman swung the screen door open again and stuck her head inside, hollering, "Kyle! Go get Hank. Tell him there's a lady here to see him." Holding the door out to Brenna, the woman repeated the invitation. "Come on in. Care for some lemonade or iced tea? I got both."

"No, thank you," Brenna returned. She'd thought about the impending confrontation for weeks. Actually, if she were to be honest with herself, she had to confess to planning her meeting with her father for years, but in recent weeks she'd decided to make it happen, and she'd mentally rehearsed her attitude. She would be totally detached, of course. He was a complete stranger to her, and she would treat him as such. Yet the moment this woman had said, "Hank's around here somewhere," Brenna had begun to feel queasy.

Everything about the house felt massive and masculine. Brenna glanced up the wide staircase and down a dark hallway as she followed the woman into the living room. She saw varnished pine paneling and polished wood floorboards, only one of which creaked. A huge, gray stone fireplace dominated the room, and a row of long, narrow windows provided natural brightness in a room filled with natural colors and textures.

"Have a seat," the woman offered. "Hank'll be in shortly. I'm Janet Hood. I'm the housekeeper here."

Brenna accepted Janet's handshake with a level stare. The woman didn't even have the grace to hesitate over the word, Brenna thought. Housekeeper, indeed. "How do you do? I'm—"

"We got company, do we, Janet?" The voice, resonant

and authoritative, preceded the man, who rounded the doorway with a long stride. "Kyle said a—" He stopped. One beefy hand, full of coiled leather, froze for a moment before dropping slowly to his side. "A lady..." It was obvious that he recognized her the minute he saw her face, and Brenna wondered, as he returned her frank stare, how that was possible. He'd seen her only as an infant. "I didn't think you'd come yourself," he said quietly. "I thought maybe you'd send someone."

Brenna was unnerved by the man's stare. He recovered quickly from his shock; now he looked less surprised than purely fascinated. He took a step closer, interest glinting in his blue eyes. "You know who I am, then," Brenna managed.

"You look just like your mother," he said. "Just as beautiful."

"You were missed at the funeral." It had taken her a moment, but Brenna was able to return the man's blatant perusal now, affecting casual interest as she realized that he looked older than she'd imagined.

"I don't think so. If Althea had sent out invitations I wouldn't have been on the guest list." He took in the whole picture of his daughter at once—the strawberry-blond hair primly fastened at the nape of her neck, the cool green eyes, the flawlessly fair skin, and the small, delicate stature—and he shook his head in amazement. "The resemblance is incredible."

"Strange you should see that," Brenna said, her voice stiffening with her back. "She often said I looked like you, though I see little resemblance between myself and either one of you. Did you get my letter?" A movement at her side reminded Brenna of her manners, and she turned to Janet with a cool but civil, "Excuse me, Janet, I was about to introduce myself. I'm Brenna Sinclair."

"I'm sorry about your mother, Brenna," Janet said simply. "I'm sure you two have a lot to talk about, so I'll just excuse myself. There's lemonade and iced tea in the refrigerator," she added, glancing first at the daughter and then the father on her way out of the room.

"Sit down, Brenna," Hank offered, using the loop of the leather strap in his hand to indicate a brown leather chair. "Can I get you something to drink?"

"No, thank you."

"I got your letter and your lawyer's letter. I also got *her* lawyer's letter." Hank took a seat on one of the sofas, and Brenna accepted the proffered chair. "You said you'd be looking to—how did you put it? Appraise the situation? I was expecting a visit from one of the attorneys."

"I decided to come myself," Brenna told him.

"Why?"

"I guess I wanted to take a look at you."

"How hard a look?" he asked, settling deep into the overstuffed sofa and folding his arms over his chest. "Are you interested in seeing for yourself what kind of a man your father is?"

His dark hair was graying, and the lines etched deeply into his face betrayed his age, but his body did not. His waist was thick, but not flabby, and his rolled shirt-sleeves revealed the forearms of a man who had worked hard. That thought came as something of a surprise. Brenna had pictured a gentleman rancher, a playboy. "Not really," she decided. "It's a little late for that. I'm interested in seeing the property I've inherited so I can decide what to do with it."

"I see." His tone was flat. "Didn't your mother leave you any instructions?"

"No. She simply left me her property. All of it." Leaning forward slightly in her chair, Brenna considered the man, his apparent strength and the will that must have been part of that strength. "I had no idea that she owned this land. Of course, it comes as no surprise that a man who married money would occupy his wife's property, but after such a long separation, why did you stay here?"

"We bought this place with Althea's money, but I built the business with my own sweat. Why wouldn't I stay?"

"Why didn't you buy her out?" Brenna asked.

"The property wasn't for sale," Hank told her, a hint of resignation creeping into his voice. "Not to me."

Brenna settled back, resting her elbows on the arms of the chair as she laced her fingers together. "Which means a divorce would have been inconvenient for you."

"And for her. We maintained separate residences for twenty-five years because Althea preferred to be married rather than divorced. I've never fully understood why," Hank confessed. "She took nothing from me but my name and my—" he saw the expectant flash in his daughter's eyes and quickly chose different words "—some measure of my freedom."

"Your freedom?" Brenna's fingers tightened against one another and the cords in her neck stiffened, but she sat perfectly still and returned his level stare. "Perhaps that was the price of the ranch, then."

"The terms of the lease, to be more exact."

"You paid rent?"

"Not in cash, but, as you say, Althea had her price."

Brenna made a steeple of her forefingers and touched them to the point of her chin. "Funny. I would have said that you had yours." Dismissing the subject as she rose abruptly from the chair, Brenna strode to a window and peered out at the pasture beyond the driveway. "I'm interested in horses," she announced, a bit unnerved by the fact that she was at a loss for something to call him, a name to attach to the end of her statement.

"Yes, I know," he said, trying to cover the pride he felt in being able to add, "I've read about you."

She turned, surprised. "Have you? Then I guess I should confess to having read about you, too. An interviewer once asked me if we were related."

"Really? What did you say?"

"Distantly," she recalled. Returning her attention to the window, Brenna continued, "I've never worked with Arabians, but I see the breed growing in popularity. It would be interesting to see the horses and something of your breeding program."

"They're *my* horses," he clarified firmly. "Your mother had no interest in them, financially or otherwise."

"I know that."

Hank stood, shoving his hands in his pockets as he approached her. "I'm surprised at your involvement with horses. I would have expected Althea to nip that in the bud."

"I attended boarding schools," Brenna explained. "Riding was encouraged, along with Latin and grace before meals."

Hank smiled, but when Brenna didn't, he told himself that his daughter was undoubtedly as haughty as her mother had been. He hadn't fought hard enough, and he had let this happen. "I understand you use some pretty unorthodox training methods," he ventured, hoping to make some contact with her on the one common ground they seemed to have.

"They're effective," she told him.

"Excuse me." Both heads turned toward the doorway, where Janet stood a bit awkwardly. "O'Brien's here, Hank."

"Good. Tell him to settle in, park his trailer by the hook-ups. I'll be with him shortly." To Brenna, he offered, "My farrier. Best in the business. He's quite a trainer in his own right, too, but he's got a thing for Spanish mustangs. Waste of time, if you ask me."

"I don't believe I've ever seen one," Brenna said, dismissing his opinion with a shrug. "I'd like to change clothes, and then I'd like to see the rest of the property. Do you have a guest room?" An invitation to stay in her own house would surely not be necessary.

"Janet will show it to you. I'll get O'Brien started in the stud barn, and then we'll give you a tour." He stopped, looking Brenna in the eye. "I'm prepared to buy Pheasant Run. You'll want an appraisal. Bring in whomever you want. I'll pay a fair price."

"Even though you built it with your own sweat?" she challenged.

"It's always been mine. All I'm buying is the deed."

"If I decide to sell," she reminded him, moving toward the door.

She walked back to the car mechanically managing not to stumble simply out of habit. Brenna's insides boiled, her head pounded, and her peripheral vision dimmed. Not one word of explanation, not one hint of regret from the man who was supposed to have been a father to her. They were complete strangers, and he accepted that as a matter of course. She'd thought that she had accepted it, too. Her mother had told her more than once that Henry Sinclair was—how had she put it? An attractive peasant. What had Brenna expected from such a man? Pretty rhetoric? That was her mother's forte. Her mother, the aristocrat. From her mother, Brenna had gotten her fill of rhetoric.

For the duration of the tour Brenna became an automaton programmed for proper civility. She dressed for horses. Her butternut breeches and a comfortable old pair of hunt boots might not be the mode for South Dakota, but Brenna dictated her own style.

Actually, she heard little of Henry Sinclair's monologue as she followed him from stall to stall, paddock to paddock. She allowed the smells of the barns and horses to fill her head, ran a practiced touch over conditioned muscle and groomed hide, and willed the familiarity of it all to restore her serenity.

"Would you mind if I went for a ride?" Brenna asked as they surveyed the contents of the tack room together. There were several kinds of saddles, mostly Western, but the hunt seat she preferred was among the collection.

"I had it in mind to take you out myself a little later. You'll want to see some of the hay land and the pastures. You haven't seen the stud barn yet, and—"

"Dad!"

Brenna jerked her head at the word which had been shouted from some distance behind her. A young man, sandy-haired and bright-eyed, clucked to his mount and cantered toward them.

"That's Kyle," Hank offered, and Brenna glanced back to catch her father's proud smile. "Come over here, Kyle. Meet your sister."

Brenna's face grew hot as she watched the slender rider leap to the ground, stuff his hands in his pockets and flash her a bashful grin.

"Kyle is my son," Hank explained. "You knew I had a son." Brenna answered with a wordless nod. "Kyle, this is Brenna...my daughter."

Kyle brushed the mop of hair away from his forehead before he stuck out his hand. "It's good to meet you."

"It is good," Hank agreed, watching the tentative handshake with an approving eye. "It's good that you two should get acquainted after all this time."

Brenna vaguely wondered why he thought it was a good thing. This was another stranger, and when she'd heard him call Henry Sinclair "Dad" she'd felt a twisting in her chest, a feeling she couldn't account for. She had nothing to say to this boy.

"Got time to take a ride with us, Kyle?" Hank proposed. "I was just about to show—"

"I'm sure you have work to do," Brenna said quickly, edging away. "And really, I think I'd rather wait awhile before I...I'm rather tired."

The berating Brenda treated herself to as she strode away from the father and his son did nothing to alleviate the chaos churning inside her. She'd known about the boy. Her mother had mentioned him in passing during one of their monthly lunches together when Brenna was in prep school. She'd given him considerable thought at the time. She had a half-brother somewhere, in addition to a father—two people who shared blood and genes and an unknown history with her. It had sparked her imagination then, but she had been safeguarded by distance and the romance of fantasy. The possible explanations behind her father's estrangement had been endless, all of them more dramatic than her mother's explanation: "He prefers to remain where he is."

As she hung her clothes in the guest room closet, Brenna reminded herself that she was here on business. Girlhood fantasies were far behind her. She owned the land these people lived on, and that land happened to boast one of the finest lines of Arabian breeding in the country. The horses belonged to Henry Sinclair, but the ranch belonged to Brenna.

Brenna was an excellent trainer. She had studied anatomy and the physiology of exercise, and developed conditioning methods that were scientifically sound, though considered somewhat unorthodox by some of the established trainers. Their skepticism had been unimportant to her, except perhaps as a factor to spur her on. She'd traveled, studied, experimented and apprenticed, and she knew horses. She wasn't interested in breeding horses for increased size or speed. Her challenge was to condition a horse to peak fitness and test his endurance.

It was the Arabians that interested her, not the man who raised them on what was now her land. He was a breeder, just like any number of others she knew. She could have sent an agent, but she had come to South Dakota to see the land firsthand because it supported a horse-breeding operation. That was the only reason.

So why hadn't she looked at the horses? Why had she allowed herself to be led from stall to stall like a zombie, and why couldn't she remember one animal she'd seen? She wasn't tired, and she rejected the thought that she might feel intimidated by anything she faced out here in the middle of nowhere.

Brenna took her black velvet hard hat from her tote bag, along with a soft pair of kidskin riding gloves. Not only would she look the horses over, she would try one out. She didn't suppose anyone around here dressed this way for riding, but she doubted that anyone around here rode the way she did. She jammed the hat firmly over her head and glanced in the mirror. Once in the saddle, she was always unflappable.

It was late afternoon. The temperature was probably higher than it felt, but the dryness and the breeze were unexpectedly pleasant. The unmistakable clang of mallet against anvil rang out from behind one of the barns. Since she saw no one in the corrals, Brenna was drawn to the familiar sound. She let herself through a squeaky gate, crossed the paddock and rounded the corner of the barn, following the noise.

The man who swung the mallet was the most powerfully built she'd ever seen. His chest and shoulders glistened with the sweat of his labor, and his muscles swelled with each stroke. Towering well above the six-foot mark, he was complemented by the handsome, long-legged sorrel stallion who stood cross-tied within a few feet, waiting for the man to shape his iron shoes.

Brenna stopped, captivated by this sun-bronzed man. He continued to work, the rhythm of his mallet claiming all his effort. His black hair curled in damp tendrils over his forehead and down the back of his neck. His black mustache formed a rakish brush over lips taut with concentration, but his chest was smooth and hairless.

The pounding subsided and he set the mallet to one side while he raised the tongs, bringing the horseshoe close to his face for examination. Brenna watched, her eyes on the horseshoe, wondering whether he was satisfied with what he saw. It was a moment before she lifted her eyes to find that what he saw was her. He stared as boldly as she did, his dark eyes piercing, one eyebrow hiked questioningly.

If his eyes asked one question, hers responded with a dozen. The churning she'd struggled with suddenly gave way to an all-over flutter that was equally foreign to her but infinitely more pleasant. She took a tentative step in the man's direction, but his eyes narrowed slightly, and she stopped short, as if she'd suddenly found herself in a pasture with a strange bull. The intensity in his eyes warned of an impending charge. Brenna stood ready, her pulse quickening with anticipation.

Then he dismissed her and turned back to his work, thrusting the shoe back into the fire. Brenna felt cheated. She clamped her jaw, biting off the greeting she'd planned to utter, and marched stiffly into the barn. There she selected a young gray stud, saddled him, and led him back into the sunlight.

"I'd choose a different horse if I were you."

It was a deep, strong, whiskey voice. Brenna turned to find that she had his attention again, but this time his eyes flashed with something like amusement. She wasn't sure, though, since his mouth was immobile.

"Why? Does this one lack spirit?"

"No," he admitted, "he doesn't lack spirit."

"Neither do I," Brenna assured him. Reins in one hand, she reached for the cantle with the other, realizing that it would take nothing short of a chin-up to put her in the saddle.

"You'd better let me give you a leg up." The disarmingly smooth voice was close to her ear. Brenna turned her head back toward the smell of smoke and damp musk, and gave him a steady, unflinching stare. He was far taller than she was, but there was stature in the green brightness of her eyes. "This horse might not stand still for acrobatics," he explained.

Any objections she might have had were lost in the sudden lift he gave her into the saddle. He held the back of her calf firmly in one hand while he placed the iron over her booted toe, then glanced up, challenging her to resist his hold. She didn't. She simply returned the scrutiny.

When he dropped his hand and turned to move away, she nudged the horse, asking for a walk. He stood his ground. The man opened the corral gate and swung his arms wide, his eyes bright with amusement. Tempted by the promise of freedom, the horse cooperated, but once through he stiffened, and his walk became a recalcitrant crow hop. Brenna sat easily in the saddle, taking control and turning the motion to a rocking-horse canter as she left the beautiful man and his smirking eyes behind, and turned her face into the wind.

"You're right about one thing, lady," Cord O'Brien mumbled as his eyes followed the awkward-turned-graceful departure. "You don't lack spirit."

Chapter Two

This woman was every inch the daughter of Hank Sinclair.
She carried her head high, just like his horses did. O'Brien
had left the gate open, and he caught himself listening for
her, glancing up once in a while toward the stretch of grass
she'd covered as she rode away. She was smaller than he
would have expected, but she had no shortage of confidence. In O'Brien's book that was a point in her favor, but
she could lose that point if he found her confidence lay
simply in the fact that she was who she was. O'Brien had
no use for blue bloods, equine or human.

He'd heard that the love of Hank Sinclair's life had been
a blue blood from back East, and that Sinclair was still
married to her. It figured. Sinclair was always talking about
bloodlines, about his Arabs being out of "Prince" this or
"Royal" that. The man had a whole damn barn full of
"Sheiks." O'Brien hadn't seen a Sheik yet who could sur-

vive a winter in the Rockies and still have the stamina to outrun grain-fed horses for two weeks straight.

He found himself smiling when he caught sight of the girl and the gray, and wondered what kind of stamina she might have. So far she was still on top of that gray.

"Why didn't you tell me he wasn't broke to ride?" Brenna demanded as she kicked her foot free of the stirrup and lowered herself to the ground.

"You didn't ask." O'Brien clipped off the end of a nail and ran his hand over the hoof before he looked up to see the woman leading the horse in his direction. "Did you lose your seat?"

"No. In fact, we got along famously after I established some ground rules. How much work has he had?"

O'Brien let the hoof down and straightened his back, feeling a twinge as his vertebrae reorganized themselves. "I don't have anything to do with the training around here. If he didn't buck you off, he must be at least green-broke. You're lucky."

Taking a step back, Brenna gave the gray another quick appraisal. "I think he'll have a nice trot when he learns to carry a rider. He needs a lot of toning, but now that he's reached his full height, he looks like he'll fill out nicely." She glanced back at the man, offering a tentative smile. "You did try to warn me," she admitted. "No harm done. It was just that I was looking forward to a joyride, and it ended up being a training session."

O'Brien raised a skeptical brow. "Old Hank's pretty picky about who does his training."

"I'm Brenna Sinclair." The name had become sufficient calling card in the horse world, but she didn't notice the usual dawning of recognition as she offered this man her hand. He made no attempt to brush off his own hand before taking hers. His clasp was warm and strong, and she felt for a moment that she'd been swallowed up completely.

"Cord O'Brien."

The name reverberated in her head, and she felt a little short of breath. "You're the farrier?"

"Yeah." He chuckled, fully aware that he was holding her hand now, not shaking it, and that she wasn't pulling it away. It was small and delicate, like a bird's wing, and he liked the feel of having it tucked inside his own. "You're the daughter."

Brenna withdrew her hand. She could imagine the talk, the impersonal references to "the daughter" and "the wife." She was the one the people who worked here had heard about, the one with all the money. "In a manner of speaking," she answered quietly, turning back to the horse.

"He showed me an article about you once," O'Brien explained. "About the way you condition horses for cross-country. Looked like an interesting method."

"Did you read it?" She ran the stirrup up and loosened the girth.

"Yeah, I read it. Might be a good idea for some of these flatland horses and the ones with all the fancy pedigrees."

"You don't like fancy pedigrees?" she asked, moving around to deal with the other stirrup.

"I don't think they mean much."

Brenna shrugged. "There are lots of good cold-blooded horses," she agreed. "Soundness is what's important." She looked up and discovered that he'd gone to untie the stallion he'd been working on. "Are you the one with the Spanish mustangs?"

"I've got a few," he told her as they led the horses into the barn.

"I don't think I've ever seen one."

"They're homely," he said. "You wouldn't be impressed."

Brenna hauled the saddle off the gray's back. They led the horses into neighboring box stalls and continued their conversation through the wall. "Are they sound?" she asked. "Your mustangs, I mean."

"Sounder than the dollar. They've been around longer."

"But they're a dying breed, aren't they?"

"The pure strain is rare," he acknowledged from his side of the wall.

Brenna unbuckled the headstall, and the young stud let the bit drop from his mouth. He was docile for a green-broke horse, she noted, rubbing the soft hair at the base of one of his smoke-colored ears. "How do you determine the purity of the strain?" she wondered absently, backing out of the stall. Turning, she came up against a hard wall of male chest.

"You know it when you see it," he said quietly. She lifted her face to him. Beneath the low brim of her riding hat those round, green eyes dominated her face. He watched her small breasts rise and fall with a quick, startled breath beneath her cotton shirt. He felt the warmth of her breath on his skin, and the sudden tightness in his own body surprised him. She was hardly what he would call sexy. In the dim light her face was bright and pearl-colored. Her skin might take on a bit of a golden cast in better light, but this was probably as tan as she ever got. She wore little makeup. On the horse's back she'd seemed to have more substance to her, but now she felt like a bit of silk brushing up against him, and he wondered how she could have controlled the untrained gray. He wondered, too, how long he could control his own urge to reach out and touch her again.

Brenna saw the urge in his eyes, and she waited, knowing that if he put his hand on her, she would, as always, move away. But his hands didn't move, so she didn't move away. She looked up at him and waited, her pulse throbbing. He was physically overwhelming—height, build, dark good looks.

"I see you've met O'Brien."

Standing in the doorway with the sun at his back, Hank Sinclair knew he'd startled the pair. They both turned abruptly, but neither saw the hint of amusement in his shadowed face. They looked as though they'd been caught at something, and Hank figured it was something neither one had made sense of yet.

"Yes," Brenna responded, and then to O'Brien she offered, "I hope I haven't kept you from your work."

"You might have slowed my progress, but you haven't kept me from it." O'Brien took his shirt from the peg where he'd left it hanging and shrugged into it, promising over the top of Brenna's head, "I'll get to the gray next, Hank. Your daughter seems to have taken a liking to him."

"You mean that old gray mule?" Hank wondered, stepping closer to the gray's stall. "You took him out?"

"I hope you don't mind," Brenna said evenly. "It didn't occur to me that you'd have a stud that old who wasn't—"

"That horse is about to become a cull," Hank explained. "Bad conformation, bad blood, bad manners."

"Oh, I disagree," Brenna said quickly. "With the right conditioning, that horse is built perfectly for cross-country. That is your interest, isn't it?"

"Endurance racing, yes. But that horse hasn't got the heart. I'm planning to geld him and sell him. After supper I'll saddle up a good horse for you." O'Brien had already started out the door. "Janet expects you for supper, boy," Hank called after him. "Said she made your favorite, whatever the hell that is."

"I asked her to boil up that dog of yours. He tried to bite me again."

Brenna found herself stepping directly in front of the door so she could watch Cord O'Brien walk away. Hank was laughing, and so was O'Brien, though she certainly had no idea why. Boiled dog, indeed. The tail of his unbuttoned shirt fluttered behind him as he strode across the paddock.

"He's part Indian," Hank explained, chuckling. "Dog-eatin' Sioux, they used to say. Hell of a good horseman."

Besides the family, which Brenna considered to be Henry, Janet and Kyle, there were two employees and one guest for dinner. For the moment, although she was Pheasant Run's legal owner, Brenna mentally conceded that she was a guest. Cord O'Brien was not at the table. The two men who worked for Henry each acknowledged Brenna with a "how-do," a question about where she was from and a comment about the heat, which, they assured her, was unusual for May. After that they were anxious to report to their boss on the day's activities. Brenna's attention drifted in and out of the table talk.

The dining room was dominated by bright light and wood. Tall windows on two sides of the room were draped in blue and yellow calico, which had begun to fade. Heavy pine furniture and a huge braided rug added to the rustic effect, and another massive stone fireplace promised added cheer on dreary days. The meal suited the decor. Thick beef stew and fresh-baked bread were served on stoneware. Drew Mitchell, one of the hired men, solemnly told Brenna that she had missed "one hell of a dinner," which had been served at noon and was traditionally the full-course meal of the day.

Brenna smiled and passed the butter to Charlie Wright,

who was older and, by his own admission, a little slower than Drew, but his experience with horses and farm machinery made up for what he lacked in agility. The men made a genuine attempt to include her in the conversation, but Brenna was well aware that she was being measured by five mental yardsticks, all of them belonging to people who had a stake in her property.

Between Brenna and Janet there passed a silent assessment. Privately Brenna admitted that, though this was her house, it was Janet's home. Brenna watched and listened as the men talked, but she felt Janet watching her. Brenna was a threat to Janet's men—the father who was no father to Brenna, and the half brother who sat at his father's right hand. Kyle was reporting on his day's work, looking to his father for approval of every detail. Henry's head bobbed as Kyle talked, and Janet, the woman whose home and family were suddenly facing an intruder's threat, sat watching and waiting.

Brenna's insides tightened when she thought of herself that way. Her appetite waned before she'd eaten much. She shouldn't mind breaking up this pretty little domestic scene, since she had no part in it. She wasn't even a hole in her father's life. Until today, she had obviously had no existence for him. But she didn't like the idea of playing the snickering villain in the black cape. She could sell him the place and wash her hands of him completely. Pheasant Run was all there was between herself and Henry Sinclair, and if he could buy it from her, that would put an end to the connection.

The back door slammed, and Janet came to life, hopping from her chair. "There's O'Brien, and everything's cold now," she mumbled, gathering serving dishes from the table and scurrying into the kitchen to replenish them.

He strode in as though this were his party, but he did

offer a perfunctory, "Sorry I'm late." He chose the chair next to Brenna's rather than the one across from her, and headed off Hank's comment. "I know, Hank. Supper at six on the nose. I also know that Janet's got a good heart, and she always keeps the pot warm for latecomers. Pass the bread."

The last was directed at Brenna, who caught herself staring and moved quickly to oblige. Covered with a properly buttoned shirt, Cord O'Brien's shoulders were no less imposing than they had been bare. He'd obviously come straight from the shower, and there was no nonsense about his scent—pure soap and water. He took the bread basket from Brenna's hand and caught her gaze again. A lock of hair, still damp, but this time from shower rather than sweat, dipped toward one smiling eye. "Thanks."

"There's hot stew." Brenna looked up and saw that Janet hadn't missed the moment. Brenna busied herself with setting the basket down, and Janet noticed her plate. "Might seem strange, serving stew on a night like this, but a working man needs a hot meal. I can get you something else, Brenna, if the stew's not—"

"Oh, no, the stew is fine," Brenna said quickly.

"I have leftover chicken, and I could make you a salad."

"No, really. I'm enjoying this, Janet. The bread is wonderful."

Janet returned to the kitchen, satisfied. O'Brien leaned closer and offered quiet reassurance. "The dog's still out back, mean as ever."

When Janet came back to the table she noticed that both of them were smiling.

"That horse O'Brien was shoeing today, that was the one you should've taken for a ride, Brenna," Hank announced from the head of the table. "Dakota Sheik. Magnificent animal. Came in fourth at Rocky Top last year. This year he'll take the cup.''

''I'd say he's too fat for an endurance race,'' Brenna judged.

''Fat!'' Hank protested, leaning perilously close to his plate. ''That horse is *prime*.'' Kyle, who'd been quiet, started to say something. ''Well, maybe not quite prime,'' Hank amended with a shrug. ''We've been putting the feed to him all winter. He needs work. But by the time that race rolls around, he'll be in top form.''

''That might take some doing,'' Brenna said. ''The gray I rode today could be in better shape for an endurance trial by then. He's got good legs.''

Henry Sinclair settled back in his chair, eyeing his daughter. ''Is there a challenge hidden in there somewhere?'' he wondered. ''Personally, I don't think any conditioning can make the difference between a mule's first cousin and a trophy winner. The gray's a cull, and I should've sold him as a two-year-old.''

''You're wrong.'' They were two words Henry Sinclair seldom heard. Brenna lifted her head and quietly added, ''About the horse and the difference conditioning can make.''

''Care to put your money where your mouth is, girl?'' One arched brow taunted her.

''I beg your pardon?''

Hank chuckled, remembering the same expression in Althea's eyes when she had said those words. ''I *said*, wanna bet?''

''Bet what?''

''My Sheik against the gray—or any other horse you care to use to prove your point.''

''For what stakes?'' Brenna asked, more curious than tempted.

"I'd put up the Sheik," Hank suggested. "He's the key to my breeding program."

"And what would I have that might interest you?"

"A deed," Hank clipped.

"You expect me to bet the ranch against a horse?"

"If I win, I expect you to sell Pheasant Run to me at a fair price."

Brenna considered the blue rose painted on the plate in front of her. "I would be more interested in the horse I won the race with than your Sheik."

"That gray?" The horse wasn't the issue, and Hank knew it, but he kept up the front.

"I could do it with the gray," Brenna returned, "if I wanted to take the time."

"Have you done much endurance racing?" Cord O'Brien put in quietly.

With a sidelong glance Brenna informed him, "I'm a professional trainer, Mr. O'Brien. I have trained and conditioned horses that later went on to become champions in cross-country trail riding and steeplechasing, as well as endurance racing."

"Have you actually participated in all these events yourself?" O'Brien wondered.

"I'm a trainer," Brenna repeated, "but I do like to compete in cross-country."

"Endurance?"

"Not—"

"Have you ever entered the Rocky Top?" O'Brien specified.

"No."

"It's a hundred-mile race almost straight up."

"I've had plenty of experience with mountain terrain."

"Air gets pretty thin at high altitudes," he warned, and

then lowered his voice, adding with a shrug, "but then, you're probably used to that."

Hank caught the innuendo and grinned. "Place your bets, boys. What kind of odds will you give me, O'Brien?"

"I'd say even money on the Arabs to place," O'Brien projected, tearing into a piece of soft bread. "I'm going to take first in the Rocky Top with Freedom this year."

"You're not actually going to enter one of those little mustangs of yours?" Hank laughed. "You're crazy, O'Brien."

"No crazier than this little flatland filly." He grinned down at Brenna. "I wouldn't want to miss seeing what ten thousand feet does to your equilibrium."

Sparing O'Brien only a second's hot glare, Brenna turned back to the head of the table. "What's the gray's name?"

"Prince Valiant." Pleased with himself, Hank chuckled. "Maybe it's an omen. If you treat him right, maybe you'll get a valiant effort out of him."

The night air was chilly and deliciously clean. The legs of Brenna's cotton trousers swished against ankle-deep grass as she followed the rail fence from post to post. She'd just come from the barn, where she'd taken another look at the gray and told herself that, yes, this horse would go the distance. Once she got her hands on him, she would build his stamina muscle by muscle, heartbeat by heartbeat.

Brenna's leisurely pace had taken her away from the house and the outbuildings, past the little trailer that was apparently the brawny farrier's summer home, and led her in the direction of a moonlit pasture and a small copse of cottonwoods near the paddocks. The riot of stars overhead and the depth and clarity of the night sky were almost overwhelming to one who had known only east-coast skies. This was her own moment with the sky. There was no one to share it with, as, for much of her life, there'd been no one to share the good moments and the bad. She smiled. There was no one around to catch her, either.

Impulsively Brenna hoisted herself up on the fence. She balanced herself on rubber-soled sneakers, arms outstretched like the tightrope walker she'd once dreamed of becoming, and negotiated the four-inch rail, heel to toe. She had a heady sensation of almost flying. It was similar to the freedom she felt when she galloped a horse. Tipping her head back, she offered to embrace the stars. A distant tinkling, like the highest piano keys, caught her off guard. She tumbled off the rail and went down, grabbing frantically for support.

Soft laughter jarred Brenna's senses when she found herself sprawled on her bottom in the grass. Braced on her elbows, she watched a figure emerge from the cottonwoods and amble toward her. Even in the shadows, she knew it could only be one man.

"I didn't mean to laugh, but that was a great move."

"You were watching me," she accused. "Why didn't you cough or something?"

Hunkering down next to her, Cord O'Brien chuckled again. "I didn't want to embarrass you. You weren't expecting an audience, and I wasn't going to let you know you had one. You okay?"

Brenna looked down at herself as if to check before giving her answer. "I think so. That was certainly stupid of me, wasn't it?"

"Looked like fun to me. Bet you're pretty good on a balance beam," he guessed.

"I *used* to be. I don't know why I decided to try to recreate the experience."

In the bright moonlight she could see his smile. He

shoved a glass in her direction, ice tinkling against the sides. "Drink?"

"What is it?"

"Ice water. Good for what ails you."

"Only if I sit in it," she quipped, and he laughed again as she took a sip. "Mmm. This tastes good for some reason." After another drink she returned the glass, eyeing him warily over her upraised knees. "I didn't realize there was anyone else out here."

"You feel like I caught you with your pants down?"

"Something like that."

"Don't worry, Miss Sinclair," he promised with exaggerated solemnity. "Your secret is safe with me. The fact that you're really human is just between you, me and the gate post."

"I have a feeling you might be the one person I'd want to keep that from."

They stared at each other for a moment before he settled comfortably on the grass. "I guess it's too late now," he said quietly. "I know what I saw." He smiled. "Kind of a nice surprise."

Brenna hugged her knees and lifted her slight shoulders in an indifferent shrug. "I have my weak moments."

"Like the one you had at supper? That gray's had very little work, you know. Hank's Sheik may be a little fat at the moment, but the gray needs basic training."

"I know exactly what he needs."

Her smile was saucy, and in the moonlight, with that pale hair falling back from her small, upturned face, she had the look of a child who was teasing him with a secret. "You planning to stay long enough to see it through?" O'Brien asked. "The race isn't until the middle of August."

"If I decide to take the bet I'll see it through. And I'll beat him."

"The stakes are pretty high for him," O'Brien pointed out, studying her now as he draped a forearm over his knee. "You're not after the horse, and the ranch is just a piece of property to you. What would you stand to gain?"

"It's a chance to demonstrate the soundness of my training methods. This is new territory for me, a new challenge, and the setting is perfect," she explained, waving a slender hand at the expanse of pasture nestled at the foot of the Black Hills.

"Whose benefit would this demonstration be for?"

"I'd keep a journal, of course. Believe it or not, the work I do generally catches a great deal of interest among horsemen, both in this country and abroad. I've worked with several excellent British trainers who—"

"Believe it or not, your work catches Hank's interest, too. He's told me about it." He caught her frown. "He likes to talk about you, but I get the feeling all he knows is what he's read. Why is that?"

"If he confides in you so much, surely he's told you that he and my mother separated when I was a baby." The idea that her father even mentioned her to people made her uncomfortable somehow. She'd assumed she was simply a dead issue with him.

"I wouldn't say he's confided in me," he said. "We've known each other for a long time, but he's never talked about his marriage. I was surprised when he told me earlier today that it was his late wife who'd owned the land. I always thought Hank's veins were actually filled with the runoff from Pheasant Run's hills."

Glancing away from his face, Brenna ignored the uncomfortable feeling she always got when her inheritance was mentioned. "My mother owned a great deal of property."

"And now it's yours," he observed, his tone matter-of-fact.

Her back straightened slowly, and she lifted her chin toward him in an attitude of defiance. "Yes. Legally it's mine."

"So what are you going to do?" he wondered. "Kick him out?"

"I haven't decided." She splayed the fingers of one hand over the grass, letting the combination of dry stalks and green tips tickle her palm. "You said he likes to talk about me," she began without looking up. "What does he say?"

"Every once in a while he'll show me an article about you in some magazine and ask me what I think."

She looked up quickly, a bit wary. "And what are your thoughts, Mr. O'Brien?"

He drained the glass and then rattled the ice a bit for effect. "I think you've got good legs. You and the gray should make a good team."

"What a clever observation," she drawled. "So full of masculine insight."

O'Brien lifted a shoulder, offering a lopsided grin. "You asked me what I thought. I figured I'd be on safe ground if I just mentioned legs. Horses I can judge in the first meeting, but women…I stick with legs until we get to know each other better. Hindquarters and chests can be sensitive topics with some women." He tossed her an insolent wink. "If masculine insight means anything, you can rest assured you've got good legs, Miss Sinclair."

She tried to glare at him, but couldn't banish her smile in the face of his, which was soft and charming in the shadows. Finally she gave in and laughed, and he joined her. In the quiet that followed they listened to the horses grazing nearby. The sound of ripping grass was punctuated by the occasional stamp of a hoof or the swish of a tail. Though horses were her life, Brenna had never known the pleasure of living with them in the backyard, and she'd never known a backyard that covered so many acres of good land as this one did.

"Do you travel a great deal in your work?" Brenna asked finally. "I see you take your accommodations with you."

"I like the feeling of having my own place," he said of the camper-trailer that was parked nearby. "Even if I can't stand up in it."

"I can't see you fitting yourself into one of those efficiency showers," she said, giggling at the mental image of him getting those shoulders wedged between two narrow walls.

"Sure you can," he teased. "Come on over tomorrow evening after I knock off work for the day." To her credit she only rolled her eyes and shook her head. "Actually the trailer is outfitted with an oversized bed and shower I can get into. But Hank's got a locker room out in the main barn, and I use that when I'm here."

"And how long are you here?"

"Off and on for most of the summer. I do a lot of work for the horse owners in this area, and Hank lets me set up here so he can kind of keep me around."

"Where's your home?" she asked, adding quickly, "Surely you don't stay in that trailer all winter."

"I have a place out in Wyoming," he told her. "Up in the mountains. It's nothing fancy. I raise a few horses."

"Spanish mustangs?" He nodded. "How do you *raise* them? I would think if they were raised domestically you couldn't call them mustangs anymore."

"Mustangs are different from wild horses," he explained, stretching out on his side and leaning on an elbow. "Most wild horses are strays or the offspring of strays. The true Spanish mustang is the descendant of the original sixteenth-century Spanish horse. Small herds of them have been found in some of the very isolated regions of the West. Those of us who are interested in preserving them have taken our breeding stock from those herds, which are quickly disappearing, even in isolation.''

"How do you know they're really the descendants of those ancient horses?" Brenna asked, her interest piqued. She liked the sound of his voice. It was low pitched, and he spoke with a mellow Western drawl.

"The characteristics have been identified. I've got a guy bringing one out here in a couple of days so I can work with him. When he gets here, you'll see they're distinctive. Feisty as hell, but once you get one working for you, he doesn't quit. He can survive anything." With a sigh he amended, "*Almost* anything. I lost my stud and most of my mares a year ago last winter in a snowslide."

"So what do you do without a stud?"

"You spend most of the winter catching another one. Freedom. That's the horse I'm bringing down here. The mares are all bred, so half his job is done. Now if I can just get that ornery cuss to carry me in the saddle, we'll be in business."

"You're entering that race with a horse that isn't even saddle broken yet?"

He laughed at the incredulous look she gave him. It reminded him of the way she'd looked at him when she first saw him.

"And you said *I* was crazy," she finished with a flourish.

"Yeah, but I didn't deny that I was, too. I just said I wasn't as crazy as you were." He laughed. "Maybe it's a toss-up. But at least I know the mountains, and so does my horse. Now, if we can just agree on who's boss, we can beat your Arabs hands down."

Brenna leaned back with a satisfied smile. "I knew I'd beat Henry Sinclair and his precious Sheik, but frankly, I was a little worried about you. Now I'm sure I have nothing to worry about."

"Oh, yeah?" He clucked softly and gave her another one of those cocky winks. "You go right on thinking that way, Miss Sinclair. Overconfidence in the opposition suits me just fine."

"Oh, I do have confidence, Mr. O'Brien," she assured him as she stood, lightly brushing at the back of her pants. "It's founded on experience. *Over*confidence tends to be a masculine trait."

Following her lead and rising, Cord had to admit that he enjoyed the advantage he felt when he stood over her. Her hair had a brightness of its own in the night, and she smelled sweet, like a woman. He was sorely tempted to take her in his arms and explore the differences between their masculine and feminine traits, but instead he chuckled softly. "Yes, ma'am, you go right on thinking that way and we'll have ourselves one hell of a race."

Chapter Three

The old man struggled to hold the pickup on the road as he stretched for the pack of Camels that had slid across the dashboard just out of his reach. The coating of dust on the dash didn't bother him, even though it was transferred to his fingers and then to the end of the cigarette he stuck in his mouth. But he did notice the effort that stretching cost him. Wet weather made his joints ache worse every spring. He lived in the mountains, where winter moved in early and melted away late. At this point in his life Jesse Pickett's creaky body needed sun.

But his spirit thrived on high altitudes, and once he unloaded these horses and hoisted a couple of beers with Cord, he would head back to his mountains. These little hills they had in South Dakota were a poor excuse for high elevation. Hank Sinclair had made it worth Cord's while to work down here, but Cord knew that need to go home to the mountains, too, and he came home regularly. He and

Cord were two of a kind, Jesse thought as he drove under the "Pheasant Run" sign. Even if they'd had blood in common, they couldn't have understood each other any better.

Jesse parked the pickup and followed the sound of the mallet, knowing full well that he would find Cord at the source. Joints cracking from the long ride, he told himself that he'd be damned if he'd walk like a seventy-year-old codger, even if he was one, but his swagger had stiffened despite his protests. He still dressed in sharply pointed boots that curled up at the toes, and he still wore his boot heels down on the outside edges. His body might have turned to gristle, but it hadn't gone to fat, and he was proud of that.

Cord looked up from where he was crouched underneath the belly of a black gelding. Kneading his back as he stood, he nodded toward the old man and took up his mallet.

"Back bothering you again, is it?" was Jesse's greeting.

"It's been giving me a little trouble lately," Cord reported, shoving an iron shoe into his portable forge.

"Better go in and have it straightened out before it gets worse," Jesse advised. Cord nodded. "Got your broomtails in the trailer. Where do you want 'em?"

"How many'd you bring? I just asked for Freedom."

"You said you were gonna enter that suicide race down in the Hills. You can't enter that bad news cayuse in any suicide race. He'll kill you for sure." One worn boot heel skidded in the dust as Jesse planted himself in front of Cord, making the younger man look up from his work. "Fact is, boy, if you've got that back trouble again, you've got no business ridin' in any suicide race, and you've got no business puttin' a saddle on that horse. Now I said my piece, and I ain't gonna say another word."

"Until when?"

"Until I get good and ready," Jesse promised. "I

brought Buckshot down. He's the best saddle horse you got, and he can beat the socks off any flatland horse in that suicide race, which you ain't got no business entering.''

"Freedom's faster," Cord said simply. Arguing with Jesse was as foolish as spitting into the wind.

"But he ain't ready, and he ain't gonna be ready, and you know it. That horse don't like you, boy. Naming him 'Freedom' don't change the fact it was you took his away, and he ain't forgettin' that. I think you oughta just put him out to stud and forget this fool notion you've got of provin' how tough he is. You and I know how tough he is. Ain't none of the horse fanciers ever gonna admit it, even if they see it with their own eyeballs. And that's all I'm gonna say on the subject.''

Cord cocked his friend a lopsided grin. "Let's unload the broomtails, old man, before you make a liar out of yourself again.''

When Buckshot backed out of the horse trailer Cord remembered how the mustang had gotten his name. He always came out of the trailer as though he were being shot out of a gun. The horse's hindquarters danced out first, with Jesse trotting after at the end of the lead rope, doing his best just to hang on. Cord laughed, but the tables were turned when he went in through the trailer's front door to battle Freedom. Gentle words of persuasion were followed by furious oaths. Jesse peeked through the side window and choked back a howl when he saw the two powerful bodies, head to head, eyeball to eyeball, each trying to muscle the other down. Man finally won over beast, and the horse backed out. The two faced off for a moment, chests heaving, before Freedom allowed himself to be led to the pens that Hank had set aside for Cord's use.

The sound of clattering hooves brought Cord's head around toward the cement walkway separating one barn's pens from another. Jesse followed Cord's eyes to the source of the sound and saw why Cord's stance reminded him of a stud suddenly aware of the presence of a mare. Every fiber of the man's being was attracted to the small woman on the prancing gray Arabian.

The horse was attuned to her, and they made a pretty pair, Jesse thought. Her gloved hands were steady, her signals to the horse invisible, but he was as attentive to her as Cord was, and Cord wasn't missing a trick.

"Who's the lady?" Jesse mumbled from the side of his mouth.

"Sinclair's daughter."

"Nice."

Cord cast a mock scowl past his shoulder. "When are you going to start acting your age, Jesse?"

"When they figure out a way to roll it back about forty years. You met her?"

"Yeah, I met her."

"And?"

"And she's Sinclair's daughter. High-headed and untouchable." Cord gave Jesse a second glance. "Come to think of it, she might be just about your speed, old man. You can't do much more than dream, anyway."

"Still got a few tricks I ain't taught you yet," Jesse clipped, heading toward the gate by the stud barn. He lifted his voice to the lady. "Let me get that for you, ma'am."

Brenna smiled and thanked the old cowboy, making every effort not to look past him as she spoke. She introduced herself, diligently filed the name Jesse Pickett with an image of the leathery face, and responded to the usual pleasantries before turning a very proper smile and a polite, "How are you this afternoon, Mr. O'Brien?" in the direction of the man whose physical presence had begun to give her strange palpitations. Heaven forbid they should become visible. She simply was not accustomed to men who didn't wear shirts when they worked.

"Can't complain, Miss Sinclair," he returned, pulling a red-hot horseshoe from the forge. "How's the gray working for you?"

"Valiant is…" The man's interest was clearly on the shaping of the horseshoe. "I'm pleased to have met you, Mr. Pickett. I think I owe my horse a rubdown."

Both men watched Brenna lead the gray into the barn. "*Mr.* O'Brien?" Jesse repeated.

"What do you expect? She only just met me."

"Sounds uppity as hell."

Cord shrugged. "I kinda like it."

Brenna eased the black hunt cap off her head and ruffled the damp hair that clung to her temples. Valiant is doing just fine, she'd started to say, and he would receive all the TLC she habitually lavished on her horses. She started by currying him briskly following with a soothing rubdown with pungent-smelling liniment that warmed Brenna's palms as she washed it over the horse's muscles. As she applied leg wraps, she went over the day's progress in her mind. She'd known this horse would respond well to her training. Within the last couple of days she'd begun to glimpse his real potential, and she was excited about it. Her progress made Kyle look like an amateur with the highly touted Sheik.

Leaning back against the wall of Valiant's stall, Brenna remembered the urge she'd had today to discourage the boy from sprinting with the other horse. She'd stopped herself. Let Henry Sinclair's son ruin Henry Sinclair's prize horse. They'd watched her work the gray at a trot. They'd conferred, and she'd seen them share a laugh as she trotted on. Walk, trot. Walk, trot. There would be weeks of that before she let him work at a canter or a gallop. No doubt the two men would share more laughs at her expense. O'Brien would probably join them. Let them laugh, she told herself. They could damn well laugh until their sides ached. Valiant would be sound when he finished the race ahead of them all.

Brenna was careful to put things away exactly as she found them. No matter what claims she had here, this was someone else's tack room. The curry comb, which could easily have been one of hers, wasn't. It was Henry's or Kyle's, and she didn't feel comfortable "helping herself," even though she'd been told to. No matter how many times she turned the words *father* and *brother* over in her mind, they continued to be just words.

What am I doing here? she wondered. I came; I saw. There's nothing to conquer. I don't belong here.

Suddenly aware that she wasn't alone, she turned and looked up. There he stood, filling the doorway with the breadth of his shoulders. He'd put on a faded red shirt, and that shock of black hair strayed over his forehead. In the dark depth of his eyes she could see proof that he'd read her thoughts.

"Am I in your way, Mr. O'Brien?"

"Not at all." She was probably in *somebody's* way, but definitely not his. As he took two steps into the small room he saw her stiffen and wondered what had happened since the night she'd taken a tumble off the fence and they'd actually shared a couple of laughs. This woman needed to loosen up a little. "You said you'd never seen a Spanish mustang."

"Is yours here?" she asked, her eyes lighting up with interest.

"Two of them. Jesse always goes one better."

"Two wild horses?" she asked, stretching on tiptoe to lift the bridle she'd used toward the only empty hook on the wall—the highest one. His hand covered hers and held it while he flipped the headstall over the hook.

"One's still pretty wild; one's as gentle as a kitten." Wide-eyed, she watched him bring her hand under his nose and touch her finger lightly to the mustache she'd thought would feel bristly. Its smoothness made her finger tingle. "Provocative scent, Miss Sinclair. The finest French liniment, no doubt."

"Of course." Their eyes locked, and his brightened, though he didn't smile. She felt the warmth of his breath and the slight stir of his lips against her finger, which she moved just enough to reaffirm the softness of his mustache. "Which do you prefer?" she asked, fascination immobilizing her. "The gentle or the wild?"

"I need both." He let her think about that for a moment before he smiled, gradually releasing her hand. "Sugar and spice."

Taking a deep, steadying breath, Brenna reached for her hat and turned to follow him. "Does Mr. Pickett work for you?"

Cord laughed and repeated one of Jesse's favorite quips. "Jesse Pickett works for *no* man." Then he added, "We're friends."

"Is he from Wyoming, too?"

"We ranch together. In fact, we built the place together over the years." Swinging the barn door open, he let her pass through first. "Jesse raised me."

"Why?" She was surprised that she had voiced the question so quickly and so bluntly. It was certainly none of her business why the man had been raised by "a friend," and he would be justified if he took offense at her prying. She found herself waiting for his answer.

"It was a tough job, but somebody had to do it," he said lightly.

"I suppose that was an impertinent question," she admitted. "He seems like a nice man."

"It was, and he is. Now come on over here and take a look at some *real* horses, Miss Sinclair."

Neither horse seemed bothered by Brenna's scrutiny. She looked Buckshot over first, then turned to Freedom. Cord swallowed his inclination to warn her against getting too close. The woman was no amateur horse fancier. She was cautious, but her manner was reassuring, and the ears Freedom initially laid back at her approach gradually eased upright. To Cord's amazement Freedom stood when he heard her quiet, "Whoa, boy," and allowed her to run gentle hands over his chest and foreleg.

"You're right, Mr. O'Brien," Brenna declared as she moved to stand beside him. "They're probably the homeliest horses I've ever seen."

"I was hoping you'd say that, Miss Sinclair. I've suspected as much myself, but it's reassuring to have a second opinion."

She looked up at him, squinting against the sun. "Why would anyone want to breed homely horses?"

"Because they're like no other breed, and they're worth keeping around." He strode over to Buckshot and led him back to Brenna. "You say you're into endurance, Miss Sinclair, and I say there's no horse better equipped to endure the hardships of a long mountain trail than this one is. Look at him." The first thing Brenna noticed, now that they stood side by side, was that the man nearly dwarfed the horse. Then she took a second look as he pointed out other features, his big hand leading her eyes from point to point. "He's short-bodied, narrow-chested, ideal for maneuvering in tight places. He carries his hind feet directly underneath him, and his tendons are tight. Look at the round hooves. Perfect for rocky paths. He's got round cannon bones, the better to absorb shock, and his eyes—see how they're sort of slanted? He can see better in front and back.

"These hairy ears may not be too pretty, but they give him better protection from insects. He turns just like that—" Cord snapped his fingers, and Buckshot pricked his ears. "On a dime."

"But he's so small," Brenna protested.

"Like the Arabian, he's only got five lumbar vertebrae, so he's short-backed, and he never reaches more than thirteen hands tall."

"I don't even see how he could carry a man your size."

"He can carry me into next month," he told her, grinning proudly. "And he loves the high country. He can find grass where you'd swear there wasn't a blade. And I'll tell you something else about these horses: they have more red blood cells than other breeds, so they carry more oxygen in their blood. When you get up there where the air's thin, you'll wish for red blood instead of blue, Miss Sinclair."

Brenna folded her hands over her chest, tucking her hunt cap under her elbow. "My blood's as red as yours is, Mr. O'Brien, and I think your horse looks like an overgrown pony."

"And I think your blue-blooded horses are headed for disaster if breeders don't get over this idea that bigger is better. They keep breeding them taller and longer all the time. 'More stretch,' they keep saying. How much can a horse stretch before he starts getting sway-backed?"

Brenna considered the argument, one she'd heard before and had some sympathy with, and she reconsidered the horse standing in front of her. It was still ugly. "Why don't you work with a more...a more acceptable breed and just select for less size?"

Cord sighed and shook his head. "You're not a good listener, but then, neither is your father." He didn't miss the icy green flash in her eyes when he made the comparison, but he ignored it and went on. "It's more than size. These animals have evolved naturally, in perfect harmony with their environment. I don't think I can do any better. All I want to do is keep them around as a reminder of what a horse is supposed to be."

"That's an interesting notion, Mr. O'Brien," Brenna decided. She looked at him with admiration. "Noble, even. But I doubt that your horse business will ever be profitable, if this is what you're raising."

His eyes narrowed in a tight stare. "I'm a good farrier, Miss Sinclair. My services are very much in demand, and I make a good living. I'm not out to make a profit on my horses."

"But of course you *are* out to make a point about them—through this Rocky Top race."

He raised one thick, black eyebrow. "Aren't we all?"

Brenna had agreed to enter the Rocky Top Endurance Ride, but not to win a bet. She didn't take betting seriously, although, from the look of it, Henry Sinclair did. The training and conditioning of Dakota Sheik seemed to occupy a considerable share of his attention. Kyle worked the horse daily, and the fat was definitely coming off, but Valiant looked better. Anyone could see that. True, he was the smaller of the two, but if Cord O'Brien's evaluation were valid, the smaller horse might have an edge in maneuverability. Valiant was eager and responsive, while the Sheik seemed complacent. He was the cock of the walk, and he knew it. The Sheik was ripe for toppling.

It was becoming easier to offer Henry Sinclair the cordial conversation that was due her host. Brenna had decided not to give any thought to their relationship, and with that in mind she could be quite civil. They had a mutual interest in horses, and they talked quite often on the subject. He seemed to let her take the lead, offering a little humor when she seemed disposed to laugh. He could actually be funny in his own way, and Brenna did laugh. Not heartily. Not spontaneously—certainly every moment with him had to be carefully guarded—but on occasion she allowed herself to laugh with Henry Sinclair.

The occasion never arose when Kyle was around. In his presence Brenna withdrew quietly into herself. It was a habit she knew gave people an excuse to label her aloof, but it allowed her to eliminate uncomfortable realities from her world. She was surprised to learn that Henry had not given Kyle his name; Kyle's last name was Hood. But that was the only favor Henry had withheld. Kyle was the heir apparent to everything Henry Sinclair had. But everything did not, at this point, include Pheasant Run.

Pheasant Run. She'd never expected its endless grassland, its rolling hills, its quick-flowing creeks and vast blue sky to become so attractive to her. The more she rode it, the more beauty she saw in this land. She loved to ride out early in the morning, when the cool air was still and the sky was newborn pink and blue. That was the time when she was most likely to come upon a flock of pheasants feeding near the creek. At her approach the birds would spread their wings and sail only a few feet above the ground, just far enough to get out of her way. She would see grouse, hear the cooing of mourning doves in the stands of ash and cottonwoods, and occasionally catch sight of a high-flying hawk, but the pheasants were her favorites.

The house was Janet's province. Brenna spent as little time there as possible, but it held one item of interest to her, and, as near as she could tell, it interested no one else. The baby grand piano in the living room was never played. She asked Henry about it once, and he had told her simply that it had been Althea's, and that he kept it tuned. "Every once in a while somebody who comes over knows how to play," he explained. "Do you?" Brenna nodded. "Have a go at it whenever you like," he offered.

Try as she might, she could not imagine her mother sitting in this room and playing this piano, she reflected one evening. Her mother had been Chippendale and Queen Anne, and this room was leather and pine. She ran one finger over the piano's polished top.

"Want a beer?" Henry asked.

"A...a what?" Was this an invitation to socialize? If so, it would be the first Henry Sinclair had extended her way.

"I asked O'Brien to come over after he's done fighting with that wild horse of his." Henry shook his head. "I never knew a man who had more love for horses or less sense about them. Most men get that way over a woman, but with O'Brien it's those damned mustangs. Anyway, everybody else has gone into town. Janet and Kyle went to see her mother. I thought maybe you'd like to join O'Brien and me for a beer, maybe a little three-handed gin."

Brenna glanced at him and then back at the piano. She felt ridiculous. She didn't drink beer, and the only card game she played was bridge. She was ill-prepared for bunkhouse socializing. "No, thank you."

When she looked up at him again she reminded him of a young girl. He'd never known a little girl, and he didn't know quite how to deal with that look. "Would it bother you if I played the piano?" she asked, her voice a soft, small thing.

"Not at all. You go right ahead."

She waited until he left the room, and then she sorted through the sheet music in the piano bench. It had been her mother's music, and now it was hers. Her piano lessons had begun as a concession to her mother's demands, but they had become a source of enjoyment. She felt wonderfully feminine when she played.

The back door rattled, and she heard men's voices in the kitchen. They would have their beer and their cards, but they would hear her music. Brenna went to her room and changed into a soft silk blouse and a black skirt. She brushed her hair and let it settle in soft waves about her shoulders. She'd showered before supper, but she'd settled for simple soap scent. Now she erased the memory of liniment and horse smells with a spritz of the scent of flowers. She was ready to make the piano sing.

Cord's concentration was shot. Whatever card was closest to his right hand went down on the table. He drained his beer, a gesture that allowed him a few seconds just to listen. The music touched every inch of his body like soft hands.

Hank broke into his reverie. "I think I'll go out to the barn for a little while. You, ah, you have another beer, O'Brien."

"What?"

"I've got some work to do," Hank said.

"The hell."

"You're not playing cards, boy. You go ahead and listen to the music. Comes a time when a man's gotta listen to the music."

Cord didn't know how much Hank had drunk, but the beer seemed to be getting to him. He had a silly, faraway look in his eye as he reached over and clapped a hand on Cord's shoulder. Deep in the pit of his stomach Cord felt a twinge of uneasiness about that look, but he dismissed it. Hank wasn't the kind who would try to maneuver a man. "Each to his own," Hank was always saying. Of course, that was generally in reference to horses.

Brenna was sitting with her back to the doorway, and she was so engrossed in her music that she didn't notice her audience. She played a hauntingly beautiful melody, and when she finished he let the last notes fade into silence before he asked, "What's the name of that song?"

Her back stiffened. She turned slowly to find him leaning a single shoulder against the doorway, a brown bottle in one hand. "'Für Elise,' by Beethoven. It's one of my favorites."

"I think it could easily become one of mine." He pushed himself away from his resting post and went to sit on the couch, a vantage point from which he could see her in profile. "Play some more," he urged.

"What kind of music would you like to hear?"

"Yours."

She turned back to the keys and played Chopin for him. It made him want to ride a smooth-gaited horse along a wooded path. She played Strauss, and he left the woods and took to the mountains, where valleys were lush with spring and snowcaps loomed above them. The funny thing was, he took her with him.

"Beautiful," he told her when she turned to him again.

"Do you like classical music?" The serenity in his face told her that he'd been enjoying it, and that surprised her.

"I liked what you played. It felt good to listen to it." He lifted the bottle of beer in her direction. "I don't suppose it's too classy to offer a beer to a lady who plays that kind of music."

She smiled. "Since you're having one, I suppose it's the proper thing to do."

"Can I get you one?"

"No, thank you."

"How about coffee, then?"

She shook her head. "Nothing, thank you."

God, this woman was hard to figure. One minute she had you thinking no man was good enough for her, and the next she reminded you of a lost child. "How can I get you to come over here and sit with me if you won't accept any of my offers?"

"You haven't offered me a seat."

He grinned, patted the space beside him, and she glided across the room to join him. He noticed the flower scent immediately and decided not to tease her about switching from liniment. Instead he nodded his approval of the femininity she'd enhanced this evening. "Very pretty, Miss Sinclair."

"Thank you, Mr. O'Brien."

"I watched you work the gray today, and I reread one of your articles on interval training for the distance runner. I think I understand it better now that I see what you're doing," he told her. "He's coming along."

"But it isn't something you'd use yourself," she finished for him. "My method, I mean."

Cord laid an arm over the back of the couch and chuckled, rolling his head back and stretching tired muscles. "Conditioning isn't what Freedom needs. His muscle tone is that of a wild horse, and with the feeding program I've put him on, there's not an ounce of fat on him. He has to be broken before I can use him, and so far his will is stronger than mine." He turned a troubled face to Brenna. "What am I doing wrong?"

He asked the question as though he truly believed she might have an answer. He wasn't patronizing her; she could see that. Something inside her felt warmer, and she let the muscles in her back relax. "You want to break him to the saddle without breaking his spirit." He nodded. "You want him to work with you instead of against you, and eventually you want him to enjoy the work." With studied interest he nodded again. "You took him away from everything he knew, and now you've got to replace that with something else."

A smile dawned in his eyes. "I gave him my mares. He seemed to know what that was all about."

"You've got to give him his dignity back, Mr. O'Brien," Brenna said seriously.

"Just how do I go about doing that?"

"By letting him know what you expect of him. By being patient with him while he tries it out over and over again until he gets it right." She leaned closer, conviction brightening her face. "You took away his freedom to run, Mr. O'Brien. Now you have to convince him that he's still free to be a horse, that what you want him to do is something horses and men do naturally together."

Cord frowned slightly, considering. "I've broken a lot of horses, and I've always known they weren't crazy about the idea. You make it sound like I should sit down and talk the whole thing over with him, like some kind of horse therapist."

Her voice rose with her enthusiasm. "You talk to your horses, don't you? How do you talk to them? 'Nice boy. Good boy. Atta boy.' Right?"

"Sure," he admitted, shrugging a little self-consciously, as though he'd been caught doing something that wasn't quite manly.

"And when they don't respond, do you...swear at them a little?"

He laughed, quite comfortable with that notion. "More than a little."

"That practice is no more effective with a horse than it is with a person," she instructed. "You need to build his confidence, both in you and in himself. You're very good with horses, Mr. O'Brien. I've watched you. But this horse has your number. You tense up when he balks with you. He knows exactly how to rattle you, and he's succeeding very nicely.''

''Jesse says he doesn't like me,'' Cord said thoughtfully. He hadn't given the idea much credence before.

''He's probably right.''

Leaning forward to plant his elbows on his knees, Cord laced his fingers together. ''He can win this race. I know he can. He can blow the rest of them away.''

''Tell him that.''

He looked back over his shoulder. ''I believe you're serious.''

''Of course I'm serious.''

''I'll tell you what, Miss Sinclair,'' Cord began with a teasing grin. ''If that horse laughs in my face, I'm coming back to you for a refund.''

''No charge for advice, Mr. O'Brien. I offer it for the horse's sake, homely though he may be.''

She had a heart-shaped face that lit up when she allowed herself to tease, even a little. ''At that rate this training business of yours isn't going to be very profitable, Miss Sinclair. I hope you've got a sideline that you don't have to be quite so noble about.''

''Touché,'' she returned with a smile, glad that her careless remark from the other day had been put aside with a casual joke.

''You're a good sport, too,'' he added. ''Offering advice to a competitor. I'll bet your conditioning would do the Sheik a world of good.''

Brenna straightened. ''Then perhaps Henry and his son would do well to reread the article, too. They haven't asked for any advice from me.''

''Hank won't, and Kyle...'' Cord lifted a shoulder.

"Kyle's a good kid. Give him a chance. That's what you're really here for, isn't it?"

Brenna returned a deliberately obtuse stare. "I came to look over the property, and I became involved in a project that intrigues me."

Cord nodded, lifting his brow in acknowledgment of the myth. "Yeah. Well, stay intrigued. I like the way you...play the piano." He smiled, hoping she would relax again. "Will you play that Elise one again?"

She returned his smile, and her face softened as she nodded.

The lilting music drew him to the piano, and he leaned one elbow on the edge of it so that he could watch her hands. Her fingers were long and slender, and she had a light, quick touch. He remembered the way she'd run her hands over Freedom, and he imagined how they must have felt. The wild mustang had stood quietly under the touch of those hands. Those hands made lovely music that swirled around in his head and made him dizzy, and one day, he decided, those hands would touch him, too.

She lifted her hands from the keys and settled them slowly in her lap. She saw his hand, dangling over the edge of the piano, and his blue-jeaned thigh, his narrow hip, the wide leather belt, his muted plaid shirt over the curve of his shoulder, his hard jaw and soft lips beneath the mustache she'd allowed one finger to test. She hesitated to lift her gaze farther because already she felt his eyes, and she knew they would pierce hers. She moistened her lower lip and took the plunge into the dark, compelling heat. She watched him lower his head, and she closed her eyes only when she felt his lips touch hers. His kiss was gentle and warm, and she had no thought of turning away.

Chapter Four

Walk, trot. Walk, trot.

"Over hill, over dale, we will hit the dusty trail…"

Collected trot, extended trot. Up, down. Up, down.

"Off we go into the wild blue yonder…"

The only people Brenna ever treated to her repertoire of uplifting lyrics were the horses she rode. People, horses—she sometimes forgot to make the distinction. Since the horses never complained about her singing, she assumed they were tone deaf.

"Hey, Brenna! Don't you ever cut loose?"

Brenna stiffened at the sound of Kyle's voice and kept her pace steady along the worn prairie grass path until he caught up to her. He trotted along beside her for a few moments, tipping his hat back to wipe his brow on his shirt sleeve before he rephrased the question. "Don't you get tired of bouncing up and down in that little dish of a saddle?"

"We call it posting, and it's good exercise, for me *and* the horse. I don't need to be bracketed in the saddle, either." She flicked a pointed glance at his heavier Western saddle, with its high pommel and cantle.

"I'll say! I'm too lazy to ride English. You must have real good legs to be able to keep that up." Kyle's laugh was boyish and good-natured.

"So I've been told."

He grinned. "I bet you have. You know, it's weird thinking you're my sister."

"Is it?" This wasn't something she wanted to discuss, but his grin seemed so innocent.

"Yeah. Every time I look at you, I think you're about the best-looking girl I've seen. And then I have to remember you're my sister, and it's weird." She smiled at him, and that gave him the courage to continue. "I guess I'd be used to it if we'd grown up together." She glanced away. "I mean, I probably wouldn't think about how good-looking you are if we—"

"Have you ever tried an English saddle?" He frowned, trying to figure out what that had to do with anything. "You'd cut down considerably on weight with an English saddle," she added.

He looked down at the saddle horn. "I don't use this one in competition. I use a lighter weight Western saddle. I've tried using that one." He lifted his chin toward her saddle. "It feels funny."

Brenna shrugged and turned her attention back to the path that wound through the draw between two gently sloping hills.

"O'Brien says you know as much about conditioning horses as—" he scrunched up his shoulders, unable or unwilling to name any names "—as anyone we know around here."

"O'Brien says?"

"Yeah. I think he's read a lot of your stuff."

"Have you read any of my stuff?" Brenna asked.

"I don't have much time for reading." He laughed at himself and confessed, "I guess I never really liked reading. I like *doing*. But O'Brien says you've got some interesting ideas."

"O'Brien has some interesting ideas, too. What do you think of his mustangs?"

"He says in the mountains they can outdistance any other breed." He tilted his head, squinting into the sun. "It makes sense, but I've never competed against one in a big trial. They're pretty small and scruffy looking, and nobody wants to bother with them much—except O'Brien. If they're all like that Freedom of his, they're not worth the trouble."

"He thinks they are," Brenna said, noting that what Cord thought seemed to be worth her own serious consideration all of a sudden.

"Dad thinks O'Brien's wasting his time." Kyle seemed to take some satisfaction in that judgment. "He says you need breeding. Just look what you've done with Valiant already. You'd never know he was the same old mule he was a couple of weeks ago. He behaves himself, and he really looks good."

Brenna slowed her horse to a walk, and Kyle followed suit. "If you stick to this pace with me, that conceited tub will start looking better, too."

"Conceited tub!" Kyle patted the Sheik's neck in consolation. "Watch your tongue, lady. This here's the next Rocky Top champion. We have just a little more fat to drop."

"He needs to turn it into muscle. Your sprinting only works the fast twitch muscles. I use a graduated program to build the slow twitch muscles first. The long distance runner needs both, you know. We're working on endurance here, not a quarter-mile race.''

"How long do you keep this up, this walk-trot, walk-trot?''

"I watch pulse rate and respiration. When a workout like this hardly changes anything, I move him into a canter.''

Kyle nodded, considering. "Sounds sensible but boring.''

An approaching rider caught their attention. Henry Sinclair rode over the hill at an easy jog and closed the distance with the graceful seat of a man who'd been born in the saddle. Brenna refused to believe this was something she shared with him. As he joined them, it occurred to her that this was the way their lives were, the three of them moving parallel to one another quite coincidentally.

"Look at that,'' Hank bellowed. "Old Mule Ears hasn't worked up a sweat. You started out early this morning, didn't you, Brenna?''

"I always do.''

"Looks to me like you're too easy on him,'' Hank judged.

"In that case, your eyes deceive you,'' Brenna informed him on a crisp note. "But then, his heart isn't visible to you, is it? Out of sight, out of mind.''

"I wouldn't say that.'' The bluster in his voice had suddenly disappeared.

Don't, Brenna told herself. You're talking horses with this man, nothing else. "What I'm saying is that your program works the animal from the outside in. I work from the inside out.''

"We'll probably both end up with the same results,'' Kyle put in hopefully. "Don't you think so, Dad?''

Hank leaned over to give the Sheik's ample rump an

appreciative pat. "It's like taking candy from a baby, son. Look what we're starting out with. In this business breeding is everything. The Sheik is foundation Arabian blood, and that's what Sinclair Arabians have come to mean." His squint gave his face a firm cast, and his judgment, like the lines around his eyes, seemed etched in stone. "You might be able to turn that cull into a passable saddle horse, girl, but not into a competitor. And it's too bad, because I would have enjoyed a good contest."

Wheeling her horse, Brenna signaled for an easy trot, tossing back, "You'll have your contest. Open your eyes, gentlemen."

Both men turned in the saddle to watch—even admire—Brenna's controlled retreat.

"Valiant *is* looking good, Dad. I never thought he could be that collected."

Henry Sinclair raised one thick eyebrow in the direction of his daughter's proud straight back. "He's looking *damn* good. But he's not the Sheik."

"Like taking candy from a baby, he says. Why do men always use that ridiculous expression? How many men have you seen walk up to some poor little baby and rip the candy out of its mouth? Good way to lose a finger."

Valiant was getting such enjoyment from Brenna's vigorous currying that he probably would have agreed to anything she said. And Cord had been about to make his presence in the barn known when the conversation got so interesting that he found himself settling a shoulder against a post and waiting. She was pretty worked up, and her bottom did a kind of hula as she worked the curry comb in brisk circles over the gray's back.

"Aren't you glad you're not a man, Valiant? You don't have to go around acting like a know-it-all to keep your ego inflated. You know what's good for you, don't you, boy? That's why you cooperate with me so nicely. What I'm doing makes perfect sense, and you and I both know that.'' She'd moved to his shoulder, and her free hand stroked his neck. He cocked one ear in her direction, letting her know he was listening to every word.

"Yes, we do," Brenna cooed softly. "*We* know, and that's all that counts. Pay no attention to those names he calls you. He thought he was going to geld you and sell you for a 4-H project. Well, he can just think again, because we're going to show them who's got the right stuff." Valiant swung his head in her direction, and she hooked an arm under his neck and laid her forehead against his round jowl. "We'll show them that you're the only one around here worth his feed."

"I hope you're referring to horses." Brenna turned quickly, a gasp betraying her surprise. Cord approached her with a teasing smile. "I can be a real bear when I'm off my feed."

"You can be a real sneak, too." She gave him a dark frown and returned to her work.

"A *snake*, you say? Them's fightin' words," Cord drawled, ducking under Valiant's cross ties and moving around to the far side of the horse. Brenna glanced up to find him watching her over Valiant's back. "You'd better be smiling when you call me a snake, lady."

"I am smiling," she said, faking it. "And I called you a *sneak*. Why don't you ever make any noise when you creep up behind a person's back?"

"That wouldn't make for very good creeping, would it? I'd miss seeing you at your best. You told me your secret was in talking nice to your horses, and now I see how it's done. You're telling him that he can do it, and I think he believes every word you say." He ran an assessing hand over the horse's hindquarters. "He's coming along nicely."

Brenna reached into her tack box for an extra curry comb and handed it up to him. "As long as you're standing on that side, why don't you make yourself useful?"

He caught both the comb and her hand in his, and he remembered how sweet she'd sounded pouring her heart out to the horse. She needed to learn a thing or two about sweet-talking a man. "Make myself *useful*? If I'm intruding I can make myself scarce."

Brenna lowered her eyes as his hand warmed hers. "You're not intruding," she said quietly. "I just... thought you might want to help."

He took the rubber-bristled comb and set to work. Brenna watched him, fascinated by the way the flat comb disappeared in his massive hand. His shirt sleeve was rolled up, and the play of muscle in his forearm was equally attractive.

"I don't mind helping, but I'm not taking over here." She glanced up and caught his knowing look. "But then, you'd never ask a man to take over for you, would you?" She smiled, and so did he. "I don't imagine you'd let me open a jar of pickles for you, or change a flat tire on your car."

Still smiling, she lifted a shoulder. "I might let you help."

"Would you let me take you out?" She gave him a blank stare, and he laughed. "I'm not after anybody's candy, Miss Sinclair. I'm just looking for a date."

"A date for what?"

"Ever been to a Western barbecue?" Brenna shook her head. "Then I think it's time you did. It's like no other party you've ever been to."

She thought better of telling him how little she liked

parties. The prospect of going to one on this man's arm was different. His eyes promised that a party with him would be different, that if she were with him, she wouldn't feel like a fifth wheel. "I must warn you, I'm not much of a dancer."

He laughed, thinking of the hula he'd witnessed only moments before. "If you've got rhythm, honey, I know all the steps."

Brenna peeled a mat of horse hair off her curry comb and dropped it on the floor before she looked into his eyes with a tentative smile. "I've got posting rhythm."

"That'll do."

Most of Brenna's clothes were tailored and functional. Looking them over, she decided that functional was a euphemism for plain. She should have shopped for something new, she told herself, something Western, like one of those denim skirts with a ruffle around the bottom. No, that wouldn't work, not on her. She was no-nonsense; she was a crisp linen suit or a... A swatch of peach-colored gauze caught her eye, and she pulled the dress from the closet. It had a scooped neck, ruffle-cuffed sleeves, and yards of fabric in the skirt. It was one of those dresses that made her feel delicate and feminine, and it was totally impractical. She wondered why she'd packed it for this trip. She'd even brought a pair of strappy heels. Holding the dress to her waist, she indulged in a fanciful twirl around the room and giggled at the thought that the heels might put the top of her head just above Cord's shoulder.

Everyone else had left for the barbecue by the time Cord knocked at the back door. He gave it two whacks and then let himself in, calling her name. Hearing her footsteps, he hesitated in the middle of the kitchen, wondering if maybe he shouldn't have come barging in. It didn't sound like she was in much of a hurry. Maybe she was mad.

"I guess I'm a little late. I'm sorry." The footsteps were getting closer, so he lowered his voice with his explanation. "I had to finish a corrective job that turned out to be a little tricky. The right front shoe had to be—"

He forgot the rest of his sentence when she appeared in the doorway. She was a vision. Her face was framed by softly curling strawberry-blond hair, and her awareness of her own beauty shone in the green luster of her eyes. He'd seen that look in other women's eyes, but never before in this one's. She'd wanted to be beautiful for him, and she realized she was. He knew that if he'd told her how beautiful he thought she was after she'd tumbled off the fence or when she chattered to Valiant while she curried him, she wouldn't have believed him. But now she was ready for the compliment.

"You look beautiful."

"Thank you." There was nothing coy or artificial about the smile she gave him. "I hope it will be sufficient distraction from the fact that I have two left feet on the dance floor."

"You could distract me from the fact that the sky was falling. And as for the two left feet—" he reached past the toaster and flicked a knob on the radio "—we'll lay that myth to rest right now."

She was in his arms before she understood what he was up to, and it was only after a few moments that she stiffened with the realization that she was supposed to step in time to the fiddle and guitar music that suddenly filled the room. He laughed at the surprise he saw in her face. He was too big to be a dancer, but he moved them both around the kitchen with effortless grace.

"What are you afraid of, Brenna? I promise not to step on you."

"I might step on you."

"I won't notice, and neither will anyone else. Relax."

"Maybe if I count…is this a two-step? If I count one two…is it three?"

"Relax first. I get to decide where we go. All you do is follow." He looked down, lifting an eyebrow. "You're not used to those arrangements, are you?"

"No, I'm not, but in the matter of dancing I'll have to defer to your—"

"You'll have to relax. Why are you so stiff?"

Because you're so close, and you're making my breath catch in my chest, and I don't usually let people get this close because I'm not sure…

"Because I'm so terrible at this," she groaned.

Don't be afraid of me, Brenna. I'm not looking for a chance to prove anything. I don't want to trip you up or take the wind out of those beautiful sails. I just want you to…

"Trust me. I'll have you ready for Gilley's before the night's over. That's it—you're catching on."

The music changed to a slower song, and he caught her close to him. "If you really want to do this right, you can put your hands in my back pockets," he suggested.

"I hope you're kidding. Where would you put your hands?"

"Around your back like this. You're too short for me to reach your pockets." She managed a little laugh and allowed him to guide her arms around his back. His boots slid against the linoleum in a step without a pattern, and her heartbeat tagged along with similar irregularity. She found her head tucked under his chin, and her brain told her that it was imperative that she breathe normally in emergencies like this. She tried.

"The key to good dancing is simply to relax and let the music and your partner carry you along," she heard him say. He held her at the waist with one hand, while his other hand smoothed the stiffness out of her back. "Western dancing isn't fancy. It's just fun."

"It seems very...physical."

"Does that bother you?"

"A little."

"It bothers me, too," he confided. "Do you think that means anything?"

"It probably means that we should...back off a little."

The song changed as if on cue. "*That* means we back off a little." He moved her to his side, holding her hand behind his back as he slipped his other arm around her waist. "This is kind of a cowboy jig." She rolled her eyes in dismay, but followed his lead. "Don't bounce too high. It's quick and easy—low to the ground. That's it!"

Cord's kitchen dance course gave Brenna the confidence she needed to brave the cement slab dance floor at the Thompsons' barbecue. Cornmeal gave the slab enough "slide" to make even her feet fly. There was a live band, complete with a fiddle, a steel guitar and a Cordovox, along with the predictable guitars and drums. Brenna was delighted with the authentic atmosphere—the covered chuck wagon, the campfire, the barbecue pit, and the plank tables covered with red-checked oilcloth.

"Half the people here are tourists," Cord told her as he handed Brenna a glass of lemonade and poured his own order of beer from the seemingly bottomless keg. "The Thompsons put these shindigs on every weekend during the tourist season. This is the first one this year, so they've invited the local ranchers to help kick things off. Look around you." He gestured with the plastic glass in his hand. "Can you tell the dudes from the cowboys?"

Brenna surveyed the crowd, mentally picking out the jeans and boots that were obviously saddle-worn. She glanced down at her dress. "I'm definitely a dude."

"But you're with a cowboy, and that gives you special privileges."

"Really? What?"

"You get to eat last, with the rest of the hands."

The chow line was forming, and the "dudes" looked hungry. Cord and Brenna bided their time. He introduced her to the Thompsons, a friendly couple who said they were glad she had come to their party and seemed to mean it. She met several other people who said "pleased to meet you" with real conviction. When Cord went back for a second beer, Brenna agreed to try some, but all the friendliness it seemed to generate didn't make it taste any better than it ever had. She traded it in for another glass of lemonade.

Brenna didn't miss the attention Cord was attracting. She remembered the first time she'd seen him, and she understood the lingering looks he got from other women. He was dressed in nearly new blue jeans and a crisp ivory Western shirt with embroidery at the yoke. His cuffs were turned up just above his wrists. Brenna was pleased that he'd chosen not to hide his thick, dark hair beneath a cowboy hat, as most of the other men had. She liked being with a man that other women couldn't help but notice.

Cord noticed that Brenna came in for her share of attention, too, his mental reply to each appreciative stare was, "Eat your heart out, cowboy."

When the line dwindled Brenna and Cord took their turn at the buffet. Bowls of salad and platters of barbecued beef had been replenished, and the smell of baked beans and charcoaled meat made Brenna's mouth water. Henry Sinclair arrived with Janet just in time to be the tail at the end of the line. Kyle brought a date, and they found room at the tables to enjoy their meal. Cord and Brenna had chosen a bale of hay spread with a colorful horse blanket, agreeing silently to take a break from the crowd.

"Have you tried these? They're a local delicacy."

Brenna eyed the deep-fried something Cord's fork was pointing to on his plate. "I wasn't sure what they were."

"Rocky Mountain oysters." He scooped one up and offered it to her. "Fried in beer batter. They're delicious."

She liked oysters. He slipped it into her mouth at the first sign of acceptance, then sat back, grinning and waiting. It wasn't an oyster, but it reminded her of one. It tasted pretty good, in fact, but it couldn't be shellfish, since none was indigenous to the Rocky Mountains. "Okay, I'm ready. What is it?"

"Thompson must have branded some calves recently," he hinted, popping an "oyster" into his mouth. "What used to be bull calves are adjusting to steerhood right about now."

Brenna swallowed. "Steerhood?"

He laughed. "Don't worry. They're too young to know what they're missing."

"And I just ate what they're missing."

"When you eat the flesh of an animal, you don't want to dwell on what it was. Ever eat rump roast?"

"That's different."

"Or liver?"

"Well..."

"Or tongue?"

"Oh, Cord, that's terrible!" But she laughed, because she loved the way his eyes danced when he teased her.

"No, it's great. You called me Cord without even giving

it a second thought. We're making progress." He offered her his fork again. "Have another oyster, Brenna."

Looking him straight in the eye, she ran the tip of her tongue over her top lip before she accepted his offering. He took a deep breath, expanding his chest to relieve the sudden pressure he felt.

After the meal most of the guests moved lethargically, like a yard full of well-fed dogs. They basked in the fire glow and sipped at their beer, talking quietly, laughing easily. An occasional cigarette flashed in the dark. Brenna had the feeling the party was nearing its end, and that came as a disappointment—a premature one. The band returned to the raised platform and struck up the music, challenging the dancers to call on their second wind.

"I believe this is my waltz, Miss Sinclair."

"I think they've all been yours, Mr. O'Brien." Taking his hand, she leaned closer to whisper, "This one is a one-two-three, isn't it?"

With a wink he reminded her, "This one is a fol-low-me." Then he swung her onto the dance floor, noting that this time it took her only moments to relax in his arms and let the music take her. She was still painfully cautious, slight and delicate in his arms, and he had an urge to put himself between her and whatever she feared. That probably wasn't possible, he told himself, since he sensed he had something to do with what she was afraid of. A deep breath of the scent of her hair intensified the urge. He would damn sure give it a try.

"Mind if I cut in?"

Brenna stiffened at the sound of Hank's request, and though Cord relinquished her graciously, he knew he would have his work cut out for him when he got her back.

Brenna felt her face grow hot, and she heaped a silent curse on her tendency to blush. Why hadn't she inherited her mother's all-occasion aplomb? She couldn't think of one chatty comment.

"I just wanted to tell you how wonderful you look tonight, Brenna."

There was real warmth in his eyes, and Brenna decided it must have been the beer. "Thank you."

"Are you enjoying yourself?"

"It's a lovely party. It was thoughtful of Cord to bring me." She took a deep breath and told herself that this was just another horse breeder. "He's a terrific dancer. I'm sure I'm just slowing him down."

"Cord usually takes a turn with every woman in the place from eight to eighty, but I don't see him doing that tonight. As a matter of fact—" he cast a pointed glance at the edge of the dance floor, where Cord stood talking to Kyle and his date "—I think he's timing me."

He considered her a moment, and Brenna thought she detected something like pity in his eyes. She wanted no pity from Henry Sinclair, and she had half a notion to tell him so. "I make you uncomfortable, don't I? You remind me of her, in a way. But your eyes are prettier. They're much softer. Ah…"

Brenna looked in the direction of Hank's "Ah," and there was Cord. She reached for him, and he smiled down at her as he whisked her back onto the floor in time with a polka. Without a word of excuse or protest Brenna found herself taking to the step like a native Bavarian.

The stars seemed to brighten as she walked with Cord. The music and the lights faded, and the night became an intimate thing. A new moon reclined in an inky sky, time meant nothing, and space was infinite.

"I like the quiet here," Brenna reflected. "I like the gentleness of the hills."

"A little further south of here the Black Hills almost

become mountains. But not quite. They're just a prelude.'' He slipped an arm around her shoulders, testing his advantage. ''You have to come out to my part of the country for real mountains.''

''I've been to Jackson Hole. It's beautiful there.'' She liked the warm feeling of being tucked in next to his side, but she felt awkward and a little jittery inside. Why couldn't she be as natural as he was?

Cord reached behind him, found her arm and guided it around his back. ''How does that feel? Okay?'' Her nod was slow in coming, but it came. ''You a skier?''

''Not much of one,'' she answered quietly.

''Neither am I. That would be too convenient. The resorts are too easy to get to. I'd rather spend weeks freezing to death up in the high country trying to catch a horse that shouldn't be penned up.''

''Why don't you let him go?''

The look he gave her said he'd thought about it, and that he still gave it some thought from time to time. ''I want to keep him.'' He chuckled and amended, ''I want him to stay. I want him to walk up to me one of these days and say, 'Cord, my friend, I've decided to stick with you, service your pretty little mares, and run my guts out for you in those crazy races.'''

Brenna laughed and permitted herself to relax. ''I did tell you to talk to him, but I didn't mean you should expect a two-way conversation. Even *I'm* not *that* eccentric.''

''Yeah, but I think you're getting to me. I may even go you one better. If I get him to talk back to me, we're taking our act on the road—the hell with Rocky Top.'' He enjoyed making her laugh, and he enjoyed laughing with her. When she bobbled under his arm he caught her closer to him, but he was still chuckling. ''Steady, girl.''

''I think we've run out of path.''

A downward glance brought him up short. She was practically barefoot, and the path had turned to scrub grass and thistles.

Even he couldn't have predicted his next move.

"Cord, put me down! I can walk, for heaven's sake." He'd managed to whisk her off the ground so quickly that she hadn't had time to dodge him. Her arms went to his shoulders automatically for support, and she looked around quickly. "Cord! This looks outrageous."

"Not to me. Does it to you? No one else is looking."

"Are you going to put me down?"

"Not in this scrub. What kind of gentleman would I be if I didn't get you safely back on track?"

Her legs were balanced over his forearm, and beneath her knees she knew exactly where his shirt sleeve ended and his skin began. "What track?" she managed to ask.

He looked down, and their eyes locked. "Remember when you played your music for me? That's the track I want to be on with you, Brenna."

His lips were a hair's breadth from hers, the titillating touch of a mustache away. She lifted her chin, and he dipped his just to test, to touch, to taste. Of their own volition her arms tightened about his neck, and he took the kiss she offered—the warm, welcoming, open-mouthed kiss that came inexplicably from the innermost part of her. She hadn't even known it was there. But he had. He'd seen it in her eyes, smelled it in her hair, and remembered the taste from before. And she allowed him to taste her again, because she remembered the taste of him.

Her fingers found his thick hair as she moved to find an easy balance in his arms. The kiss became hot and moist, his tongue letting her feel what he needed, hers drawing him deeper in response. It was only when they were both dizzy with the effect of holding something in reserve that they let the kiss end.

Brenna dropped her head to his shoulder and took a deep breath, searching for her senses. "I think... please put me down now, Cord."

In two strides they were back on the path that had taken them away from the lights and the crowd. "Now that we're back on track, how about another date?" he proposed, unwilling to relinquish his hold just yet. "I'm competing in a suicide race this weekend."

He was still carrying her, walking slowly. "I don't think I want to watch you commit suicide. When are you going to put me down?"

"When you give me an answer."

"Yes! I'll go. Now, please..."

He let her slide along his body until her feet touched the ground. Now they both knew just how much he'd enjoyed that kiss. He kept her close a moment longer, taunting them both. It was good to want something that wasn't so easy to get, something that was worth waiting for. He didn't want to take her, to force her. He wanted her to give. He would earn her trust.

Chapter Five

"You ever seen a suicide race, Miss Sinclair?"

"No, I haven't." Brenna smiled past her shoulder at the old man, whose leathery frown could have intimidated a jungle cat in a stare down. "From Cord's description, it sounds as though it'll be fun to watch."

"Fun to watch unless there's somebody ridin' whose neck you don't care to see get broke," Jesse grumbled.

"You must have just about broken your neck getting back here to go to this race, old man. What time did you say you left home?" Cord grinned over the pickup's steering wheel as he negotiated yet another Black Hills curve. The grin wasn't for Jesse. It reflected the fun he was having manipulating the floor shift with Brenna's legs angled around it.

"I didn't say," Jesse reported. "And I didn't say I cared whether anybody got his neck broke, either. Just thought I'd warn the lady. These things get pretty rough." He shook his head. "This boy's got a hard head, but, big as he looks, he's got some other parts on him ain't no stronger than yours or mine." Leaning forward, he raised a gnarled index finger along with his voice. "Parts which I ain't mentioning because I been told enough times to mind my own business—" he turned toward Brenna "—but parts we all know about, and only a fool would ignore."

Brenna turned questioning eyes in Cord's direction. "I thought you told me never to discuss body parts in mixed company, old man."

"I ain't discussin', I'm just sayin'—" Brenna's hand received a fatherly pat "—that if you've got any gentle feelin' for this boy, ma'am, you better harden your heart. He's liable to be dead by nightfall."

"Dead?" She looked at Cord as though he might already be gone. "I was just beginning to like him, too."

"Don't take it too lightly, ma'am. Suicide's the proper name for this fool race. Bein' the only family the boy's got, I figured I oughta be here to claim the remains."

"If I had a superstitious nature I might worry about being jinxed," Cord put in as he parked in a field full of pickups and horse trailers. "If anything happens to me, I'll know who to blame."

The three of them eyed the vertical drop-off that was the last obstacle before the finish line. "Yessir," Jesse said. "Suicide's the proper word."

They'd brought both Valiant and Buckshot, and they'd arrived early so that Brenna could ride along as Cord reacquainted himself with the course. Brenna acknowledged that it was a rough four miles, with several rocky climbs, a steep slide into a river, brush-covered flatland, and that formidable drop-off just before the finish.

"In another few weeks Valiant could take this," Brenna

judged, "but he's not ready yet." Eyeing Cord's smaller, chunkier mount, she added, "Are you sure *he* is?"

Cord urged Buckshot into a trot as they headed up a rocky slope. As she followed, Brenna noticed the mustang's complete willingness to take the hill. He wasn't picking his way or trying to break his gait. Valiant wanted to lunge ahead, and Brenna had to hold him back, but Buckshot took the hill without stumbling.

From the top they could see most of the course—the river, a hairpin S-curve that wound among some boulders, and the flat. "Once we're out of sight head for this hill; you'll be able to see a lot of the race from here. I'll show you another spot just north of here. From there you look down on the finish line." Adjusting the brim of his hat, he looked across at her and laughed. "You sure are tall in the saddle, ma'am."

She brushed an errant strand of hair away from her mouth and let the breeze take it as she laughed, too. For once he was at her eye level. "A man your size needs a Clydesdale, Mr. O'Brien. I repeat: are you *sure* that overgrown pony can tear around these hills with you on his back?"

"Sure as I'm sitting here, I know this horse is stronger than yours." He pointed with conviction to the small, stocky bay beneath him. "Look at him. He topped this hill, then looked around and wondered where the mountains were. You just watch him work this course. Double his stamina and you'll have some idea what Freedom's going to be like."

"What about you?" she asked more seriously. "What are these weak body parts Jesse was talking about?"

"Do I look like a man with weak body parts?" Shaking his head, Cord clucked to his horse and started down the hill. "Old Jesse is just feeling his age. He'd like nothing better than to enter himself."

"So would I," Brenna called after him. "But I'll get my turn in August."

No fewer than a hundred horses assembled for the start of the race, but Brenna had no problem picking Cord out from the rest. He was the big man on the small horse. More than that, he was the standout in a jostling crowd primed for action. He'd left his cowboy hat in the pickup, and his black hair caught the sun's brightness and glinted with it. He wore faded denims and a red shirt that had seen better days.

Buckshot was keyed up, and Cord held him away from the rest of the pack. He wasn't worried about getting off to a fast start. He would make up time on the course. In the few tension-filled moments before the race began the trick was to keep fifty hot-blooded male horses from brawling over the fifty or so mares in the pack. Buckshot was a gelding, but it was spring, and he hadn't forgotten the scent of mare.

Cord thought of Freedom when he heard the high-pitched warning of a randy stud somewhere in the pack. The wild stallion would have been a handful right about then. Buckshot laid his ears back. "Steady, boy. You've got a race to win." It wouldn't be so bad in August, when the mares weren't in season.

Valiant stood quietly as Brenna leaned forward in the saddle, watching horses and riders chomp at the bit, real or imagined. She knew the tension in Cord's stomach because she could feel it in her own. He was ready; the horse was ready. The signal was overdue, but when it came the pack shot forward, bumping, stretching out, jostling for position. Brenna watched as Cord cut away from the others. His strategy now would put him in a position to use his horse's strengths later.

When the herd thundered out of sight Brenna headed for the first vantage point Cord had shown her. Several other mounted spectators obviously had the same plan. The rest, including Jesse, would drive to another observation point and come back for the finish. Brenna knew she would have the more spectacular view, and she hurried to get her place.

The Cheyenne River ran below her hill, and the place where the course crossed the river was the width of a superhighway and deep enough that the horses had to swim part of the way. She heard them coming before she saw them careening across the brush-covered flat heading for the fifty-foot slide into the river. The herd was a few contestants thinner. Amid the clouds of dust she finally picked Cord out by his red shirt as he traveled abreast of the pack. Several of the horses refused to step off the bluff, but Buckshot hardly hesitated. There was no vegetation on the face of the bluff, and the riders were all but lost in the dust until the steep grade dumped them into the river. This time there was no way for the horse to refuse. Buckshot took the plunge like a boy cannonballing into his favorite swimming hole.

The current swept them at an angle, and they emerged several yards downstream. Cord had crossed the river in the saddle, but just before they reached the shore, he pushed off to Buckshot's left, giving the horse a wide berth as both of them heaved themselves onto the riverbank. It was an advantage most of the others didn't give their horses, and many of them lost footing on the first try and fell back into the water. Buckshot shook himself like a huge dog, and Cord stood back, dripping. Brenna laughed aloud at the sight.

Now Cord was among the leaders. Brenna noticed one

young woman, who rode a handsome Arabian gelding, had taken the river in good time and was out in front. Soon enough Brenna would be doing that. She saw herself in the coming competition, and her heart pounded with the image.

The course funneled the riders onto a narrower path that led to a steep uphill grade. Cord couldn't afford to get caught behind any stragglers at this point. One rider cut ahead of him, but Cord regained his position by sailing over a patch of brush. From there Buckshot shifted into hill-climbing gear and gobbled up the grade. Brenna was impressed; the little horse could have been part mountain goat, except that he carried his rider effortlessly.

She watched until Cord was out of sight, then headed for the second vantage point he'd shown her. From there she could see the stream of contenders—a small bunch in the lead, and succeeding bunches, still hoping, followed by fading stragglers, still trying. Cord took a wide berth wherever possible, choosing untried ground over the well-worn path. Apparently the mustang needed elbow room. Leaning forward in the saddle, Cord freed Buckshot's hindquarters, and the little horse devoured another steep uphill grade, assuming a healthy lead. The flat-topped hill was a runway for the grand finale: the plummet to the finish line. Buckshot plunged headlong down the last of the course, and the rest of the herd thundered behind like buffalo driven over a cliff.

Cord had tried to maintain the wide berth with this plunge in mind, but his closest competitor took the same tack. In the swirl of dust Brenna discerned nothing about the rider except that his mount was black and was veering sharply in Cord's direction, apparently out of control. The black took a sudden tumble, and Buckshot was the only domino in his path. Paralyzed, Brenna watched the collision and the dusty slide as the riders hurled themselves clear of the churning hooves. Then she lost sight of Cord.

Valiant leaped forward at Brenna's frantic signal. A draw separated her from the fallen riders, but she thought she might be closer than the spectators at the finish line. Later she realized that the deadfall at the bottom of the draw had provided the first jump she'd taken with Valiant, and that he'd taken it like a champion.

She got to Cord first. Someone else was dragging the other rider to safety, but Cord had managed to throw himself a few yards clear of the path. Both horses had recovered, and the last of the riders were taking the slide with less zeal than the leaders had shown. Brenna slid down from the saddle beside the man who should have been preparing to collect his trophy. Instead he lay belly up in the dirt, one arm draped over his eyes.

"Cord, are you all right?"

He lowered his arm and looked up at her. God, what a beauty! She was silhouetted against the sky like some guardian angel, puzzling over him with a worried frown as she swept a stray wisp of hair behind her ear and leaned closer to his face. He'd wanted to impress her, and now he was about to make a fool of himself, at the mercy of the pain that always reduced him to a quivering baby.

"Not exactly."

"What is it? Do you think something's broken?"

"No."

She continued anxiously, as though she hadn't heard him. "Can you move? I mean, do you think you could…if I could just…" Sitting on her heels, she reached for his shoulders, then drew her hands back in premature frustration. "I probably can't."

"What? Pick me up off the ground?" She looked irresistible, sitting there fretting over him. If he could have sat up, he would have kissed her. All he could manage was half a smile. "You talk about back strain, honey..."

"Oh! Is it your back? Don't move." But he was trying. "Cord! Please, don't." She glanced down the hill and caught sight of two men and a stretcher. "Help's coming. Paramedics, I think."

He had to roll over and get up on his hands and knees, and she wasn't helping any by trying to push him back down. "I don't want to be carried down this hill. Jesse'll never let me hear the end of it. Help me roll over."

"If it's broken..."

"If it's broken I won't get up. Come on, Brenna, help me get started."

The strain in his face told her the start he'd made was costing him dearly. She offered a hesitant push, which seemed not to help at all. He stiffened and groaned.

"Hey, lady, is he okay?"

Brenna craned her neck toward the stretcher bearers behind her. "I think his back..."

"Yes!" Cord hissed through his teeth. "I'm okay."

"If he's okay we'll take the girl down first," one of the men suggested as they trotted past.

"Take the girl," Cord instructed over his shoulder, and then quietly told Brenna, "Put one hand on my shoulder, the other on my hip, and push both ends at once."

Brenna complied, and together they got him on his hands and knees. Pain shot into his buttocks and up to his shoulder blades, and he willed himself not to fall.

"Now what?" Brenna asked, hovering over him helplessly.

"You never did say whether you had any of those gentle feelings for me."

"What!"

"Gentle feelings." He concentrated on his hands and his

arms, his thighs and his calves. They would get him up. If he ignored his back, the rest of his body would get him up. "If you've got any, drag 'em out and give me something to lean on."

"Oh, Cord, this is ridiculous. You…Jesse's coming."

"Not till I'm on my feet." He did it mentally first, knees first, then one foot, then two.

"Cord…" But she was already under his arm, struggling with him, bearing as much of his weight as she could manage. "That's it," she said. "Careful."

The pain cut his back in two and ran down the backs of his legs. He was blind with it, but he was standing. He knew the moment Jesse bolstered him on the other side, though the old man didn't say a word. He wouldn't, not when Cord hurt this badly. Not when he knew Cord needed superhuman strength just to put one foot in front of the other.

When the paramedics returned he succumbed to the pain and allowed himself to be carried to the pickup, where, lying in the back under the shelter of a pickup topper, he protested against the need for a doctor.

"How many times has this happened to me, Jesse? It's just back strain. I threw it out again—that's all." He glanced Brenna's way, surprised by the anxious look he found in her eyes. "It's nothing new. I've got a bad back. Just takes a few days to get me back on my feet."

Brenna looked to Jesse for some sign of sense. "How far away is the nearest doctor?"

"Ten miles or so," the old man reported.

Cord knew he was beaten. "They can't do anything."

"One of these days they're gonna put you under the knife, boy."

"Not today."

"Today they're gonna see if you've done somethin'

more serious than usual," Jesse told him. "You wanna ride up front, ma'am? We'll slide the back window open so's we can holler back at him once in a while."

Brenna shook her head. "I'll ride in the back."

The X-ray machine at the small clinic in Custer got a workout that day. The young woman whose horse had collided with Cord's had a fractured wrist and a badly broken foot. Cord had no broken bones, but the doctor described the muscles in his back as "a pile of knots" and told him that he would be looking for disk surgery one day. Cord accepted the usual prescription for muscle relaxants and assured the doctor that he'd been told all this before.

Doc Holden had seen a lot of battered cowboys. There wasn't a bone he hadn't seen them break, or a muscle he hadn't seen them stretch to the point of ripping. They never listened. They hobbled on their way with as much dignity as they could muster and never quite let themselves heal before they tried to ride something else that didn't want to be ridden. True to form, O'Brien, stiff-backed as a zombie, insisted on walking out under his own steam, and Doc Holden followed. In the lobby he spotted what he was looking for—a young woman with an anxious look in her eyes. Their women all had the same look. No point in giving his instructions to anyone but her.

"If this man doesn't take up a different hobby, he's going to have to take up a different trade." The doctor pushed his white coat back and planted his hands on his hips as he assumed a stance of authority. Brenna stood, glancing from the shiny-pated doctor to Cord and back again. "Even I know you have to be able to bend over to shoe a horse. Now I suppose, if you baby him along for a while, he'll be back to normal in a couple of weeks. Miracle of it is, he didn't break anything, but he's got what we in the medical profession call a bad back."

Hearing Cord's derisive snort from behind, Doc Holden jerked a thumb over his shoulder. "He calls it that, too, but he refuses to take it seriously. But you," he added with a nod, "you look like the kind of woman I can count on to take it seriously for him. He shouldn't climb on another horse for at least six weeks."

"Six weeks!"

No one attended to Cord's protest. Brenna's eyes were on the doctor's face, and Jesse, in a corner chair, was all ears. "Don't let him tell you he's all right, because he isn't. He should be flat on his back in bed, or flat on his face in a dead faint. You get him home and alternate ice and heat, and don't let him overdo the pills."

"Look, Doc, she's not my—"

"Not your boss. I know." He smiled at Brenna. "You and I know different, don't we? See that he stays off those horses."

Outside in the parking lot Cord grunted as he relied on the strength of his arms to pull himself into the bed of the pickup. He couldn't lift his legs anymore. "Let's go home, Jesse."

"You don't mean all the way to Wyoming," Brenna protested, following him. "That's ridiculous."

"Not as ridiculous as it would be for me to duck into that trailer."

"We're going back to Pheasant Run, Jesse." Jesse gave her a wink of approval as he closed the hatch on the topper. "You'll stay in my room—the *guest* room, and I'll take the trailer."

She tried to help him situate himself, ignoring his expletives and cringing sympathetically when he lay back in the carpeted pickup, where they'd improvised a pallet for him with horse blankets and a folded Pendleton. From what he'd told her, she knew it had to be over three hundred miles to his ranch, and they were only fifty or sixty miles from Pheasant Run. She sat cross-legged, leaning back against a saddle, and watched him, waiting for more protests. Each bounce of the pickup postponed them a little longer. It wasn't until they reached the highway that the road was smooth enough to allow him respite.

"I really don't want to go back to Pheasant Run like this," he said quietly.

"I understand that," she said. She'd never liked sympathy, either. "I'll see you're left alone."

"What makes you think I want to be left alone?"

She eyed him cautiously. "I'll see you're not bothered, then."

"Aren't you going to follow the doctor's orders?"

It was hot. Brenna leaned over to slide a window open, and then she reached across him to do the same on the opposite side. The pickup bounced, and she felt his hand on her knee. When she looked down she saw that he wasn't making a pass. He was trying to brace himself. It made her uncomfortable to know that here was a man who seemed to need something from her. Worse, she felt an impulse to give.

"His orders were for you to follow."

He squeezed her knee. "Who better than you to give me the hot and cold treatments?"

"I'm not much of a nurse." She sat back, her legs tucked under her bottom, and avoided his eyes. "But I'll do what I can...for your back."

"I've seen you rub Valiant down." His voice had gone low and husky. "Can I expect at least that much?"

"If you don't mind my brand of French liniment."

He pulled his face into a tight smile. "It's Jesse's brand, too. Cured all my childhood ailments."

"Except your bad back," she reminded him.

He nodded. "Except my bad back, which is strictly an ailment for adults. Damn," he swore, sucking in his breath. "I don't need this now."

"I'll work your horse for you."

He frowned up at her. "Freedom?"

"He'll be ready by August if you are," she promised.

"I couldn't let you do that."

"I'll give him the same workout I give Valiant. I play no favorites in training."

He shook his head. "It isn't that, Brenna. He's a mustang, and he's really only green-broke. I don't want you on him."

"You don't think I know what I'm doing, either, do you?" she asked quietly.

He saw the hurt in her eyes, and it surprised him, because he hadn't meant to put it there. "You know what you're doing, but Freedom isn't a pasture-bred horse. He's got a wild streak in him that—"

"You don't want to take out of him, not completely." She smiled. "I do custom training, Mr. O'Brien. You'll still have your mustang."

"What do you charge?"

"What do you charge for dance lessons?"

He returned her smile. "Are you trading your favors, Miss Sinclair?"

"If you want to call it that."

"What I want to do is put in a bid for something else."

"Before you start bidding, let me warn you that I've been thinking over your advice about getting into a sideline that I don't have to be noble about."

Remembering, he chuckled, and she laughed outright. She felt comfortable now. She'd offered him help with his horse—something he needed, something she knew she could give.

* * *

Brenna's room was a good place to put an invalid. The other bedrooms were upstairs, and the kitchen and dining room were on the other side of the house. Her room benefited from morning sunlight and evening quiet. *The guest room,* she corrected as she tapped on the door. This was not her room.

"Cord? It's Brenna. Janet found a hot-water bottle."

There was a long pause, and then he said, "Come on in."

"Are you decent?"

"No, but I'm covered."

She went in quietly, as though she wanted to avoid disturbing his rest. He was covered to the waist by the bedding she'd slept in the night before, though there was no pillow under his head. His feet extended beyond the bottom of the bed, and his brown chest was bare. He turned a slightly drawn face in her direction, and she saw that he looked as uneasy as she felt.

"How are you feeling?" she asked, approaching the bed slowly.

"Stupid," he told her. "How about you?"

"I'm...not feeling any way. I'm just..." He filled the room. She was so absorbed in the way he looked, lying there in her bed, that she didn't even feel herself standing there, separate from him. Then she remembered what she was there for. "Hot and cold," she explained, extending first the hot-water bottle, then the ice pack.

But he ignored what was in her hands, and his eyes smiled at hers. "Really? Both at once?"

"I mean, that's what I brought you. Do you think we should try hot first?"

"By all means."

Setting the ice pack aside, Brenna debated with herself about where to sit, then told herself that the edge of the bed was the obvious choice. "It wasn't this hard before,' she mumbled, frowning.

He chuckled. "Never said I was easy, Miss Sinclair, but I can be had."

"I meant the bed." He wasn't funny.

"Oh, that. Hank stuck a sheet of three-quarter inch plywood under the mattress. It's supposed to be good for me."

"So's this." He glanced down at the hot-water bottle and then back at her, waiting. Taking a deep breath, she placed the rubber bottle next to him. Something fluttered in her stomach. "It's very hot. I wrapped it in a towel so it wouldn't scald you. You'll have to lift yourself up."

"I can't." He raised an innocent brow and shrugged a shoulder helplessly.

"All right, then." With another fortifying breath she bent over and reached around his waist, pushing the hot water bottle from the other side. She managed to get it under him and both arms around him, but her nose was only two inches above his belly. He smelled like Ivory soap. She glanced up the length of his chest and met his eyes. "How's that?"

"You've been working pretty hard. Why don't you rest a minute?" He knew he was tipping her studied balance, and he enjoyed it, despite the fact that he was straining his back to accommodate her hands. He even regretted it when he felt them slip out from under him.

"Twenty minutes of this, and then we switch," she announced, straightening herself.

"I don't know if I can do it any other way just now."

He *was* funny. Brenna folded her arms in front of her and tried not to let him know she wanted to laugh. "You're not going to make this indelicate situation any easier for me, are you? What happened to the *gentleman* who treated me so gallantly on our first date?"

"He fell off a horse. Pain drove him crazy." Tilting his head back, he tried to get comfortable. "Don't pay any attention to anything he says."

It was too late for that. His suggestions had already created some powerful images in her mind. She scooted away to the edge of the bed. "But if there's anything he wants, I'll be glad to—"

He caught her hand as she stood. "I want twenty minutes, Brenna." She didn't tug, but she didn't sit, either. "Talk to me for twenty minutes. Talk my back into relaxing." He was doing it to her. Her hand curled around his as her shoulders dropped. "It works with your horses," he reminded her.

"You're not a horse." She sat back down on the bed, turning to face him.

"I'm beginning to think I'm built like one—the ones that are bred for size and end up getting sway-backed."

"How did you manage a shower?"

"Jesse helped me, so I wouldn't get your pretty yellow sheets dirty. It was his parting favor. He figures I'm in good hands." He filled his lungs and gave an exaggerated sigh. "He's headed home."

"And you wish you were, too."

"Yeah." With a quick smile, he squeezed her hand, which he'd kept in his to keep her next to him. "Your good hands notwithstanding. I'd like to slink back into the privacy of my own cave to lick my wounds."

She understood. She remembered how she'd hated being hurt or sick when she was younger, because there had been no place to go but the infirmary or the dorm. "It would have been a difficult trip."

It would have been an impossible trip. Getting back to Pheasant Run had been sheer torture. He'd almost blacked out taking a shower. Only as long as he lay perfectly still was the pain bearable. "I should have bunked in with the hands."

"Janet agreed that this was the best place for you. It's quiet and private." She read his next protest. "And I don't mind sleeping in the trailer. A bed's a bed, as far as I'm concerned."

He moved his thumb in slow circles around the pulse point in her wrist. "It had already occurred to me that I wouldn't mind having you sleep in the trailer." There was no smile in his voice, and none in his eyes. "With you in it, I have a feeling a bed wouldn't be just a bed."

What he was causing with his thumb was just friction; that was all it was. She turned her head toward the dresser, and her eyes managed to find the clock. "Twenty minutes of heat," she remembered. "We should switch to cold."

"No." Her eyes swung back, and he caught them with his. "Don't go cold on me now."

"It's part of the treatment." She slid her hand out of his and reached for the ice pack.

"It's the part I don't like." When he'd first taken her in his arms to dance with her, he'd felt her resistance. It hadn't been something she'd dreamed up just for him. It had been automatic. He'd felt her fight it, willing herself to relax in his arms. And when he'd kissed her the other night, she'd melted for him. "I don't think you like it, either."

"Like it or not, Cord, it's what the doctor ordered." With great care she exchanged the hot-water bottle for the ice pack, continuing with her line of impersonal conversation. What *she* didn't like was the unnamed urge she felt. "Your muscles must be tied up in knots from trying to protect those vertebrae, which probably aren't lined up quite right or something. We have to persuade them...did you realize you were bruised here?" She touched the purpling skin just above his hip bone, then drew her hand back quickly.

"Yeah. I think I first realized it when I slammed into a rock." He caught her hand again and put it back where it was. "Your hand feels good, cool."

She let the heat from his body seep into the palm of her hand. It was a peculiar intimacy, one that promised to heal both the wound she saw and the one he didn't. "It's a wonder you didn't break any bones," Brenna said quietly, feeling the urge to let her hand move over him.

"It's a wonder you haven't bolted out of here." Before she could take her hand away again, he put his over it and pressed gently. "But you haven't. Your eyes tell me that you want to touch me, Brenna. I've seen you look at me that way before. What are you afraid of?"

Her eyes darted to the window. "This is hardly…"

"Considering the shape I'm in, this is hardly risky."

"I'm not afraid of you, Cord." Her breathing wasn't as steady as she would have liked, but she looked straight into his eyes. "You've kissed me."

"Yes, I have. Now you kiss me."

She studied his mouth for a moment, unaware that she sucked her bottom lip over her teeth and then slowly let it slide free. He saw the slight tremor in her breathing as her eyes flashed the message that the deepest part of Brenna would kiss him gladly. He had only to free that part, and she would come to him. He made up his mind that in time she would do just that.

"I'll…get your supper. You must be very hungry."

Reluctantly he let her hand slip away and watched her hurry out the door.

"No hungrier than you are, Brenna Sinclair. No hungrier than you," he said quietly once she had gone.

Chapter Six

The alarm clock shrieked in Brenna's ear. Groping in the dark, she knocked it from the shelf over the bed, and it clattered, still shrieking, to the floor. Right in her ear, for heaven's sake! It was still dark, and she couldn't remember where the light was. Hanging over the side of the bed, she fumbled with the alarm, then found the lamp switch. Eyes shut tight, she let herself fall back on the bed again.

Five a.m. There was no earthly reason why she couldn't sleep another hour.

Yes, there was. She wanted to try Freedom out. Then she wanted to give Valiant his morning workout in time to be handy when it was time for Cord's breakfast. She would be able to tell him that she'd gotten started already, and he would feel good about that. The poor man deserved to feel good about something.

Brenna stretched her arms above her head and thought that the bed was bigger than she would have expected to find in a trailer this size, but it would have to be. Cord was big. The bed left little room for anything else in the back room, and the bathroom, which was large for the size of the trailer, left only enough room in the front end for a small stove, a half-size refrigerator, a few cabinets, and a tiny table. It wasn't a home for receiving guests, but it gave Cord a place to hang his hat. In fact, there it was on a hook above the bed. His bed. Wrapping her arms around herself, she pictured him there, and her skin tingled.

Brenna made it out to the paddock by daylight. First she put Valiant through a few of his paces. She would work him again later in the day. They were becoming a team, responding to one another like two parts of one being. Henry Sinclair would eat his words, Brenna thought. If he had any sense he would have them for breakfast that very day and get it over with.

Freedom was another story. He eyed all human comers with the same disdain. That was the first thing Brenna dealt with. She spent time letting him adjust to the sound of her voice and the touch of her hand. She promised him that he would like her saddle better than Cord's, because it was lighter and so was she, and told him she would let him take her into the hills, where they could find cool water and grass no man had stepped on. She would let him be the best he could be, she said, and they would come to trust one another. By the time she rode Freedom through the last of the paddock gates, Brenna knew that it would be so.

Cord had already refused breakfast once by the time Brenna appeared at his bedroom door. Kyle had helped him up off the floor after he'd tried to get up on his own. That humiliation had left him in no mood for the food Janet had offered him. Flat on his back again, he eyed Brenna's familiar-looking tray with exactly the same look Freedom had given her earlier.

"How are you feeling this morning?"

"Have you gotten any reports?" he grumbled.

"Just that you're probably hungry and possibly a little grouchy."

"I'm a lot grouchy, so you'd better take your basket of goodies somewhere else."

"I've got nowhere else to take them," she said pleasantly, setting the tray on the nightstand. "No one else wants them."

"I find that hard to believe." He wondered if she intentionally left him openings like that, maybe looking for compliments. His back hurt, and he wasn't up to witty conversation this morning.

"Everyone else has eaten. We're lucky they left us a couple of eggs and a slab of bacon."

"Us?"

"I thought I'd join you. I haven't had time for breakfast yet myself."

He watched her fuss over the tray, examining the food for a moment as though making sure it was what she'd ordered. Then she settled on the edge of the bed. The scent of the wildflower perfume she wore only when she remembered didn't hide the distinctive odor of horse, and he might have smiled at the image that called to mind if he'd been in a better mood. Her hair had probably been clipped back on her nape earlier, but she'd brushed it out. Her riding breeches and hunt boots told him where she'd been.

"Did he give you any trouble?" He decided to see which was her stronger instinct, honesty or pride.

"Who? Freedom?" She spread jelly on a piece of toast, then sucked a taste of it off her finger. "He saw no reason to give me trouble."

"You must not have taken him out, then." Out of the corner of his eye he saw the plate; he smelled the bacon and heard his stomach rumble. Maybe he was about to learn something about his own instincts. "Forget it, Brenna. I can't sit up; I tried."

"No need for you to sit up. I'm going to help you."

"No, you're not. I feel like a fool, not being able to get out of bed this morning. I sure as hell don't want to lie here and be fed."

As she dipped a spoon into the scrambled eggs she smiled. The hot and cold packs had created a touchy situation, but she was on safe ground with food. "I could've sworn you enjoyed being waited on last night. Can you turn your head toward me just a little?"

The smell of food filled his nostrils. Something about a woman offering nourishment to a hungry man suddenly seemed natural to him, and he complied. While he ate she told him about Freedom's workout—a short one to start out with, but he hadn't fought her, once they'd found a comfortable balance on the bit. There was something about him that felt different, she said.

"He's wild born and mountain bred," Cord offered. "We all want a piece of that spirit, probably because it went out of us long ago. But something in our brains remembers."

"I'm sure you're closer to that than I am," she said lightly. Returning the spoon to his mouth, she found it closed. He stared at her, waiting. "You are mountain bred, aren't you?"

"Yes." What else am I, Brenna?

"And wild born," she added, her eyes full of innocence. "Henry attributes your finesse with horses to your Indian heritage."

"What's so wild about that?"

"Well, you know…" The spoon was still poised in front of his mouth as she cocked her head in expectation. "As an Indian, you're expected to be a little on the wild side."

"Am I?"

"I don't mean wild in the sense of dangerous." His eyes were dangerous, she realized. His eyes told her that if she expected dangerous, he might give it to her just on principle.

"Then what do you mean?"

Brenna took a deep breath, considering. "I mean like a wildflower, or a…a wild horse. You're expected to have a free spirit."

He watched her for another moment, then finished his eggs and bacon in silence. Brenna wondered what she'd said, what she'd done, but she said no more until he was finished. Finally she offered him juice through a straw. "I'm sure you'd like the coffee," she said quietly. "Strong and hot. But I don't know, unless we could sit you up somehow…"

He spared her a small smile. "Leave me wanting something. I need the incentive. Otherwise I might decide this is the only way to fly." A couple of sips of juice were about all he'd seen her take, and now she was returning plates and utensils to the tray, obviously finished with them. "I thought you said you were having breakfast with me. Are you dieting or something?"

"Of course not. I was eating, too. Didn't you notice?"

He noticed how her shoulders had sagged just a little, and how her voice had become small and hollow. She'd hit on his one cherished sensitivity, and he'd let his back stiffen automatically. A foolish reaction, he told himself. His back was already stiff enough. "I guess not. I probably didn't leave you much. Guess I was hungrier than I thought."

"And not really that grouchy." Her smile was tentative, her eyes soft and green. He wanted her to touch him, to lay cool hands on his back.

"My mother was Sioux," he began, his voice low, as though he were confiding in her. "I've got her coloring, her eyes, her hair. My father worked on the railroad. I never knew him, but he gave me his name and his build. Whatever I know about horses came from Jesse, along with the roof over my head and the clothes on my back." A smile crept across Cord's face as he remembered. "He wrestled me through school, fed me twice as much as any one kid ought to be able to eat, and gave me some very solemn lectures on the facts of life. I think he really believed it all came as a complete surprise when I was twelve years old."

It was a story he told easily, and Brenna listened, but she was remembering, too. She recalled the pamphlets she'd read, the speculations, the creepy feeling she'd had at first when all the "facts" finally jelled in her mind and she realized what all those drawings of organs and passages and ovals with tails added up to. She remembered trying to tell her mother that her body was changing. She knew the changes were normal, but they didn't feel right, and she wasn't sure they were supposed to happen just yet, because the other girls hadn't noticed anything—at least, they hadn't said anything.

Her mother told her that it wasn't something one discussed, and Brenna knew then that it had to be disgusting. When she had her first period she handled it herself without saying a word to anyone. In time any fears she'd had were laid to rest by finding explanations in books.

As Cord talked she tried to imagine Jesse's presentation. She wished she had been there.

"Old Jesse hasn't changed much in the last eighteen years," Cord said. "He's convinced all his good advice was wasted on me, though, since I haven't 'found myself a good woman to settle down with,' as he says.''

"And why haven't you?"

He raised an acknowledging brow. "I've run across a good woman or two, but I usually end up taking the high road, while they take the low road." He chuckled, pleased with the reference. "And they probably end up getting to the altar before me, but I'm in no hurry." He caught her hand and gave her a teasing grin. "I can't be. Indians used to offer horses in payment for a wife, and I've got the ugliest bunch of nags this side of hell.''

"That's probably what you'll get for them, too. An ugly nag.''

"Probably." He let his fingers stir inside her palm, and his voice roughened. "Probably get one that wouldn't rub my back for me even if I hadn't been able to change positions for a week.''

"Less than a day," she corrected.

"Seems like a week. You try lying on a board without moving for a week. See how you like it.''

Brenna filled her lungs slowly, trying to regulate her breathing as she surveyed his torso, which was a beautiful bronze, in contrast to the yellow sheets. "I don't suppose you have anything on." She hoped she sounded sufficiently flippant.

"I'm wearing a sheet and a damned fine bedspread.''

"Nothing else?''

"Uh-uh." He drew her hand to his shoulder and held it there, promising softly, "But once you flop me over on my belly I'll be harmless. You can tempt me all you want then.''

"Tempt you! I came in here to feed you and tell you about Freedom and see if I could do something to...''

He was grinning, the light from the window dancing in

his eyes as he kept her hand anchored to his shoulder. "You can. You can roll me over, lay me down and rub my back so I won't end up with bed sores."

"It would serve you right," she mumbled, avoiding his eyes in the hope of suppressing a smile.

"You're beautiful when you nag. I'll hold onto the sheet so you won't accidently get flashed."

But turning him over was not a joke. In the middle of the process she felt him quiver under her hands, and when he groaned with effort she knew it wasn't from wanting her. Neither of them thought about sheets then. Pain shot through him, and she felt it and shuddered with it. She found herself leaning over him, her cheek against his shoulder, listening to his labored breathing.

"Are you taking those pills?"

"No." The word was a grunt.

"Shall I get you some?"

"You can get me a shot of whiskey and a hot, wet towel."

Within moments she was at his side with both. "The towel's really hot. What shall I put where?"

He wanted the towel on the lower part of his back and the whiskey in his churning gut. Both proved soothing. "Don't ever tell anybody you saw me drink whiskey through a straw," he muttered finally.

"I can't imagine who'd be interested in a tidbit like that." The bed gave a little with her weight as she sat beside him. "I've never done this, Cord. What if I hurt you?"

"You can't. All you're going to do is knead me a little."

"What?"

"Like dough."

"Oh. Knead you." His back was broad and muscular, tapering to a lean waist. Where was the weak link? There was no visible flaw. "Maybe we should bring a doctor out here, Cord. Really. This much pain…"

"I hope I didn't go to all the trouble of turning over for nothing. I'm waiting for a back rub."

At first she felt completely inept. He was no horse, and she was far from unaffected by him. But then she let herself feel the satin of his skin under her fingers, let the warmth of him warm her, and the hills and valleys of him intrigue her. She tested the effect her fingertips had, first with a soft touch, and then trying firm strokes against the resistance of his knotted muscles. She thought she felt them give a little, and she went ahead with more determination.

Moving from his shoulders down the length of his back, she finally tossed the cooled towel aside and got on her knees to straddle his buttocks and allow herself to minister to the lower part of his back, which she knew to be his Achilles' heel. The sheet had slipped well below his waist, but that no longer mattered. She had no idea how long she worked over him, but her own hands ached when she finally stopped kneading and simply ran them over him as a mother would her child, letting him know she was still with him.

"This would make one hell of a picture," he said.

They'd been quiet for so long that his voice startled her. "What?"

"You in your riding boots, and me…"

She giggled and swung her leg across him with the grace of a horsewoman. Without missing a beat she had shifted back to the edge of the bed. "We probably couldn't sell it to *Horseman* magazine."

"No, but I can think of a few who'd pay top dollar, which is what you could get if you went into the massage business, Miss Sinclair. Think you could keep this up for a couple more hours?"

"Would it help?"

He groaned, this time with satisfaction. "It couldn't hurt."

She began to rub him again, easily now, and she liked the feeling. She didn't want to stop. "What happened to your mother, Cord? How did you end up with Jesse?"

"We'd lived with Jesse for about a year when she left us both. It was a neat trick; I think my father taught it to her."

"You never knew him?"

"Uh-uh. Hardly even knew her. Is that what you call a 'free spirit'? If it is, I don't think it has anything to do with Indian or non-Indian, motherhood or apple pie."

"What about fatherhood?" she wondered. It didn't occur to her to take her hands away from him now. She saw something of herself in the things he told her, felt a part of the story.

"I don't know. As I said, mine skipped out on the job."

"Mine did, too."

There was a long moment of silence, and then a quiet, "Yeah, I guess he did."

"I don't think 'free spirit' and 'irresponsibility' are necessarily synonymous," she decided. "It was good of Jesse to agree to keep you. How old were you then?"

"I was eight. I doubt that he agreed; I think she just left. And I think he loved her first, and then came to love me." With his eyes closed he thought about that for a moment, as he had so many times in the past. He hoped a lot of Jesse had rubbed off on him. "It all happened a long time ago. She died years later, and we buried her, Jesse and I. We did right by her, he said. She wasn't to blame. If he can believe that, then so can I."

She knew she'd eased his pain. His face was turned toward her, and his eyes stayed closed as long as she kept making circular patterns on his back.

Content, he let his breath out in a long sigh. She stirred him and soothed him, both at once, and it was good, he thought. Damn good.

The comfort she brought him came back to her. It soothed the stiffness in her own muscles, and it took the edge off her hesitancy. She looked at his face, the tousled black hair, the mustache and the stubble of a beard, which were purely masculine, and the long, straight, spiky eyelashes that threatened to soften the strong planes of his face. His breathing had become shallow, and the hand that lay palm open next to his side twitched a little. He was asleep, she thought. Under the ministrations of her hands he was asleep.

Without thinking Brenna leaned down and touched her lips to the middle of Cord's back.

The following day Cord saw a chiropractor, who gave him the news that he had a bad back and then proceeded to try to push things back into line. In another day he was on his feet, gingerly walking to the barn. He found his anvil right where he'd left it, and it felt good just to run his fingertips over the surface, worn shiny from his toil. Hearing hoofbeats, he cocked his head in their direction.

Brenna rode Freedom through the gate, saw Cord and smiled. Freedom was having a good day, and Cord was here to see it. She slid to the ground and led the horse to his owner. "You look as though you'd like to take up that mallet today."

"I would, but I'm going to give it another day or two." She was dressed much as she was every day, in a sleeveless blouse, riding breeches and black hunt boots. She was flushed from her workout, and Cord liked seeing her this way. He imagined himself licking away the tiny beads of perspiration that hovered on her upper lip.

Brenna found it easy to smile at Cord, because he smiled back at her as though he'd just been thinking something pleasant about her. "You should give it more than a day or two, I think. You don't want to rush it and let me win the Rocky Top trial by default, do you?" she challenged.

Cord gave his head just a hint of a shake as he shifted his attention and approached Freedom slowly. The horse's nostrils widened at his approach, but there was none of the usual balking. One point for the new trainer. "How are you, boy?" Cord asked, softening his voice for the horse's benefit. "Did you have a good run this morning?"

"Actually, no. We're not even ready to extend the trot." Brenna ran her stirrups up and loosened the girth on her saddle. She found little sweat under the sheepskin, which was a good sign. "He's an excellent prospect for interval training, though. His respiration and pulse rates are well ahead of most beginners."

"He likes to run," Cord said flatly.

"He likes to run free," Brenna corrected. As Cord tried to follow her movements she noticed how restricted his own were. Rather than turn at the waist or neck, he turned his whole body. "But today he didn't seem to mind taking me for a little jog." Freedom swung his head in her direction, and she slipped into horse talk, rubbing him behind one ear. "I didn't say you were crazy about it, Freedom, just that you didn't mind. Later we'll go out again, just for a little while. We'll go back up on that pretty hill, and we'll listen to our bodies again just to see if…but I owe you a rubdown, don't I?" She glanced up at Cord with an impish grin. "I promised."

"Oh, yeah?" Cord turned toward the horse. "How'd you manage that, Freedom? Fall down a hill, did you? Well, lemme tell you boy…it's worth it. This lady is magic.'' His glance met her eyes. "She blushes, too," he said quietly. "I don't see too many blushes anymore. You can have your bed back tonight, Brenna. Unless, of course, you've become attached to mine, in which case…''

"In which case you can stay at the house until you can bend your back." Leading Freedom through the open barn door, Brenna passed into the shadows as she tossed back over her shoulder, "You're still as stiff as a poker, Mr. O'Brien."

Standing there in the sunshine, he thought about that for a moment, then groaned inwardly. She didn't know the half of it, but Freedom soon would, if he were any kind of man at all. Cord chuckled to himself, realizing that if Freedom *were* any kind of a man he'd have to step over Cord's dead body before he got a rubdown from Brenna.

Cord knew Brenna was right. He wasn't up to doing any bending, but as soon as he had any range of movement at all, he would have to get back to work. Like any good horseman, Hank was fussy about his horses' hooves, and the Sheik, for one, was ready to be reshod. Cord would have to get an assistant to work with him for a while, someone to get under the horse and follow his directions. When Kyle rode the Sheik in from his workout Cord had him lift the horse's hooves, and his suspicions were confirmed. Dakota Sheik required corrective shoeing for a slight tendency to toe in, and it had been Cord's practice to keep a close watch on the condition.

Looking the horse over completely, Cord was struck by the contrast between the Sheik and Valiant. The Sheik was a good-looking animal, and in the show ring he would be considered a prime specimen. But he wasn't as hard as Valiant was now. Valiant carried no spare flesh. The Sheik's coat glistened, and his hindquarters were rounded, the way a halter judge might like them to be. He was rich horseflesh, "royal," as Hank was fond of saying. Hank was hung up on breeding, which was probably why he'd gotten himself hung up on a woman who was out of his league. Sure, the Sheik was out of Valiant's league, too, if they were headed for the show ring. But Valiant was getting in shape for endurance.

Cord chose the time after Sunday evening supper, when conversation lagged and coffee cups needed refilling, to mention Brenna's achievements. It was the hired hands' day off, and the small talk Drew and Charlie usually contributed to the table was sorely missed.

"Have you taken a close look at Brenna's 'old mule' lately, Hank?" Cord waited for an answer while Hank took several quick sips of coffee.

"Walk by his stall every day." Hank eyed Brenna as he sipped again. "He's looking damn near respectable."

"If that's your highest compliment, I accept it," Brenna said stiffly.

Cord figured he was the only one at the table who could justifiably be stiff. He decided it was time everyone else loosened up, and getting a few compliments rolling might be the way to make that happen. "She's done some kind of voodoo on Freedom, too," he offered. "He doesn't growl at me anymore."

"I don't care if he growls, whinnies or sings 'Dixie,' O'Brien, that jughead of yours will *never* look respectable."

Cord laughed, but Brenna saw no humor in the remark. "He'll perform," she promised. "He'll be in peak condition, and he'll work with his rider. He'll give Valiant a good contest."

"For a distant second, maybe," Hank mumbled.

"Your Sheik is going to make a fool of you," Brenna

said, her tone matter-of-fact. "He's not a runner; he's a strutter. Put him in the show ring and he'll bring home ribbons."

"He *has* brought home ribbons. He's the best-bred horse I've ever owned."

"He's fat."

Hank leaned on his elbows and laced his fingers together in front of him. His eyes glittered with the pleasure this bout gave him, but his daughter didn't know him well enough to read his expression. She returned a look of hard defiance.

"Fat comes off," Hank pointed out.

"If you know how to take it off. Kyle doesn't seem to."

"I do. Kyle does what I tell him."

Kyle shifted uncomfortably, making the wooden slats in his chair creak. "Actually, Dad, I've been watching Brenna, and I thought I might try—"

"Our methods are tried and true," Hank told his son. "We'll let Brenna train her horse her way, and we'll do things our way, and we'll see who—"

"I think I know all about your way of doing things." Brenna's voice was icy, and the sound brought all heads around. "You turn the responsibility over to someone else. You're one of those free spirits the West is so proud of breeding, aren't you? Your methods are tried and true, all right." A quick glance around told her there was no one at the table who understood what she was talking about. Henry Sinclair could do no wrong here. She moved quickly, hoping to make a clean exit before her control broke. "Excuse me."

Cord made the first move to follow her, but Janet stopped him with a hand on his. Her eyes pleaded with Hank. "Go talk to her. Tell her—"

"There's nothing I can say." He sounded like a man who'd just taken a fist in the gut. "Her mother's dead."

"Don't talk to her about her mother," Janet urged. "Talk about *you*."

Hank left the table and strode purposefully from the room. He overtook Brenna in the living room, where she was standing by the piano, having realized that the guest room wasn't hers anymore, and that she'd ruined her "clean" exit. "Brenna, we have to talk. We should have talked long before this, but I thought I'd let you get used to me first, and then maybe..." He stood over her and burned with the urge to put his arms around her. She was twenty-six years old, and she looked like a young girl, her eyes full of defiance and hurt. He sighed, his arms at his sides. "Truth is, I didn't know what to say, and I still don't."

"Why didn't you come see me, just once?" Her voice was quiet but steady, and she denied herself any tears. She allowed him a moment to answer, but he let it go by. "Why didn't you call, or write, or send me a Christmas present or a birthday card? Some girls'—" she took a deep breath. "Some girls' fathers sent flowers, or money. Some—the lucky ones—got airline tickets. They got spring break, or even a whole summer. I got camp. I got monthly luncheons with Mother. I got—" the next breath was shaky, but fortifying "—I got a note when I went home that said Mother was in Europe."

"I'm sorry, Brenna."

Yes, there was sorrow in his face, but that wasn't enough. She waited for some words. She wanted an explanation. She wanted him to say that he couldn't have done any of those things because he was a prisoner of war, or had amnesia, or a witch had turned all his men into pigs and kept him on her island for ten years. She would have accepted anything, but he only shook his head and sighed.

"Sorry? Is that all? You know, my mother didn't like me very much, and I always assumed it was because she didn't like you. I thought I reminded her of you. I tried to please her, and when that didn't work I said to hell with it and tried to please you." She drew her shoulders back, staring him down. She was stronger than he was. She could see that now. He looked like an old man. "Now I please myself. I'm very good at what I do, and I don't need your approval or anyone else's."

"No, you don't," he agreed quietly. How had he missed seeing himself in her? She loved what he loved. Why hadn't he seen that that was no coincidence? He had stopped angling for Althea's approval long ago, had let her have her life in return for the privilege of having his. Their daughter was the price he'd paid. Althea's reports had led him to believe that Brenna was happily ensconced in her mother's gilded bosom and had no need of him. It was a belief that had allowed him some measure of comfort.

"So go ahead with your training program, you and your son and your precious Sheik. You've kept your counsel to yourself, and I'll return the favor." Her eyes burned, and she was short of breath, as though she'd been running. "Just remember, Henry Sinclair," she snapped as the inevitable tears welled in her eyes. "This is my property. After all these years I've got something *you* want."

With that she whirled away from him and made her way to the guest room, closing the door firmly behind her. She would not cry, she told herself as she headed for the bathroom. She tried cold water, then hot, but her face just got redder and the tears kept rolling. A knock at the bedroom door made her groan.

"What?"

Play The Lucky Hearts Game

and get... FREE BOOKS, a FREE GIFT... and MUCH more!

Twenty-one gets you
2 FREE BOOKS and a
FREE MYSTERY GIFT!

Twenty gets you
2 FREE BOOKS!

Nineteen gets you
1 FREE BOOK!

TRY AGAIN!

The Silhouette Reader Service® — Here's how it works:

Accepting your 2 free books and mystery gift places you under no obligation to buy anything. You may keep the books and gift and return the shipping statement marked "cancel." If you do not cancel, about a month later we'll send you 6 additional novels and bill you just $3.12 each in the U.S., or $3.49 in Canada, plus 25¢ delivery per book and applicable taxes if any.* That's the complete price and — compared to the cover price of $3.75 in the U.S. and $4.25 in Canada — it's quite a bargain! You may cancel at any time, but if you choose to continue, every month we'll send you 6 more books, which you may either purchase at the discount price or return to us and cancel your subscription.

*Terms and prices subject to change without notice. Sales tax applicable in N.Y. Canadian residents will be charged applicable provincial taxes and GST.

If offer card is missing write to: Silhouette Reader Service, 3010 Walden Ave., P.O. Box 1867, Buffalo NY 14240-1867

BUSINESS REPLY MAIL

FIRST-CLASS MAIL   PERMIT NO. 717   BUFFALO, NY

POSTAGE WILL BE PAID BY ADDRESSEE

SILHOUETTE READER SERVICE
3010 WALDEN AVE
PO BOX 1867
BUFFALO NY 14240-9952

NO POSTAGE
NECESSARY
IF MAILED
IN THE
UNITED STATES

"It's Cord."

"I'm sorry. I'll let you have the room back in just a minute."

"Mind if I come in?"

"No, I...yes." It was too late. Brenna emerged from the bathroom just as the door closed behind him.

The sight of her tears tore his heart. She wore a sheer pink blouse and white slacks, and the flower scent she'd used before she came to supper greeted his nose as he approached her. "I thought you might need a backrub or something," he said.

"I'm acting silly, Cord. Please go away."

He slid his fingers into the hair at her temples and combed it back slowly. "I like you best when you act silly. I also like it when you let your hair down like this and put on a pretty pink blouse and that flowery perfume."

His whiskey-smooth voice was a balm. It seeped into her brain and took her reserve away. She lifted her chin, closed her eyes and let the tears roll. "I didn't want to tell him those things," she whispered.

"I know." He drew her head to him and laid it against his chest.

"I lost my temper. Oh God, I let him see."

"I don't know why you waited so long. If I ran into my father after all these years there'd be hell to pay."

"Why?" she asked, sniffling. "What good would it do now?"

"It would give me a lot of satisfaction. I got a little taste of it listening to you. Didn't it feel good to tell him off?"

"No," she declared stubbornly. "It felt awful."

"Well, it felt good to me."

Brenna leaned back and looked up. "But he's your friend."

"Your father or mine?"

"My...Hank...*Henry Sinclair*."

He smiled and wiped the wetness from her cheek with his thumb. "Hank *is* my friend, but I think his daughter is going to be my friend and then some. Seeing you hurt makes my blood run hotter."

"I'm not hurt," she insisted, swiping at her other cheek with her hand.

"Neither am I. I should be back in the saddle tomorrow."

"Don't be ridiculous." She slipped her arms around him and splayed her fingers over his back. "You're as tender as a newborn baby back here."

His mustache twitched with his smile as he lowered his hand from her face to her shoulder and let the heel of his hand slide over the upper swell of her breast. "So are you," he whispered. "In here. Don't try to tell me different. You're tender, and you're beautiful, and it makes me want to kiss you."

Her heart fluttered under his hand, and she wondered what he was waiting for. "Why don't you?"

"Because, Miss Sinclair, you are too damned short."

That drew a smile from her. She pulled him across the room to a small footstool that stood by the room's only chair. She stepped up on it and turned to him. "Now why don't you?"

His mustache tickled her skin as he took great care in positioning his mouth over hers. She felt his warm breath, his lips, his tongue, and then the pressure of his strength centered squarely on her mouth. She allowed her tongue to touch his and put her arms around his neck, pressing herself fully against him. He felt good, and everything inside her sang his praises.

He wanted her then and there. Her back felt slight under his hands, and her waist was a feminine curve. He slid both hands over her bottom and pulled her tightly to him, letting her know, letting her feel how hard he was. She moved her hips back and forth just slightly, and his groan harmonized with her whimper. He kept one hand where it was while the other stole quickly to her breast and touched her there. Through two thin layers of fabric her breast responded readily, stiffening and exciting him more. He knew why she needed him this way now, and he knew he couldn't do her need justice tonight. But, God, she felt good!

Her mouth was the first thing he relinquished, but her breast was still so close, so soft, so anxious for more. Laying his cheek next to hers, he closed his eyes and drew one shuddering breath. "I want more than that, Brenna."

She gripped his shoulders as if she were drowning and he were all that could save her. "Cord..."

"I want you on that bed with me."

"Yes."

"And I want to do things..."

"What things?"

"Shall I run down the list?"

He heard her quick intake of breath and felt her nod against his cheek. He buried his nose in her hair and put his lips close to her ear. "Right now I couldn't manage half of them, and the rest wouldn't be up to par. But I want you, Brenna." He looked down at her so she could see it in his eyes. "God, how I want you."

"Does your back hurt much now?"

He gave her a half-smile. His back was only part of the problem. He wasn't going to make love to her to fill a void somebody else had left. When they made love—and they would, he promised himself—he would fill a space for her that was his alone. "My back hurts like hell," he told her, knowing she needed to hear that, "but the rest of me feels great."

"Oh, Cord, I'm sorry." Stepping down from the stool, she moved away from him. "I don't know what I was thinking."

He caught her hand as she slid away. "You know what *I* was thinking, though. I want to touch you the way you touched me the other night."

"That was purely therapeutic."

Pulling her back against him, he hooked an arm around the front of her shoulders. "Like hell. We're going to cut through all barriers, Brenna, and we're going to find each other, just you and me. I promise." He dropped a kiss in her hair and whispered, "Good night."

"Where are you going?"

He was headed for the door. "I can handle the trailer tonight."

"And I'm supposed to sleep on a board?" She edged her way past him and beat him to the door. "Not on your life. Besides, my toothbrush is in the trailer. I'll see you at breakfast."

The house was quiet, and Brenna hoped she could slip through the kitchen and out the back door without another confrontation. She almost made it. "Brenna?"

Turning, Brenna saw Janet emerge from the dark dining room. Her hair was loose, and it softened her face, making her seem younger than she'd looked to Brenna before. Brenna turned from the door and waited.

"He hurts as much as you do, Brenna. Believe me. He's afraid to show it, but he does."

Brenna said nothing. Her relationship with her father wasn't something she wanted to discuss with Janet.

"Give him a chance, Brenna. It's what he's hoped for for so long, and now that it looks like he might get it, he doesn't know how to act."

"Do you know why?" Brenna asked, and before she

could take the words back she asked, "Can you tell me why there was never so much as a post card?"

Janet shook her head slowly. "It isn't my place. He doesn't blame you for the way you feel. He feels it, too. Regret, terrible, terrible regret. Help him get past that."

"Help *him*!"

"Yes, help him, Brenna. He knows he failed you, and he's sick with it. You're like him in so many ways, but you're stronger. I doubt that you've ever failed anybody."

Hank Sinclair needed somebody to talk to, and that somebody was Cord O'Brien. He could see the light under the bedroom door. O'Brien was still up. He wouldn't mind sharing a drink with a friend, Hank decided, and rapped on the door.

"Yeah?"

"The bar's open, O'Brien. C'mon out and have a drink."

Cord took a deep breath. He'd lain flat on his back since Brenna left, getting the rest he needed from his shoulders to his butt, with a long expanse of backache in between. He didn't know if he wanted to listen to Hank right now. He couldn't think of too many excuses that would change anything. Still, he'd known Hank a long time, and that was the part that bothered him. Hank was a good man. Cord rolled over on his side, eased himself up and left the room.

"What'll you have, O'Brien? Whiskey?" The bottle sat out on the bar, and from the looks of it, Hank had already had some. Cord nodded. "Some nights are whiskey nights, and this is one of them. Straight up?" Again Cord nodded. It was better than those damned pills.

They sat across from each other in big, overstuffed chairs near the cold hearth, one lamp casting their faces in soft light. They dangled their glasses over the arms of their chairs and eyed each other. This was to be a man-to-man.

"What do you think of my daughter, O'Brien?"

It wasn't Cord's way to answer a straightforward question with another question, though the words that came to mind were, "What do *you* think of her, Hank?" But he answered, "I like her."

Hank nodded, considering his glass. "She's beautiful, isn't she?"

"She's beautiful," Cord confirmed.

"You like her, and you think she's beautiful." The eyes he raised to Cord's were a father's eyes—protective, suspicious. "That bedroom door's been closed a lot lately, with the two of you on the other side of it."

Cord let the accusation hang in the air without comment.

"I suppose you think I've got no right," Hank said.

"It's a little late, Hank. She's grown up without your protection."

"You're right," Hank agreed, nodding. "You're right. I just don't want to see her hurt."

"You saw her hurt," Cord said. There was no emotion in his voice, no judgment. Let Hank be his own judge, he thought as he filled his mouth with the bitter taste of whiskey.

"I know," Hank sighed. "I'm the one who hurt her. I know."

"What are you going to do about it?"

"I'm gonna do the only thing that makes any sense," he said, swirling the whiskey around in the bottom of his glass before draining it completely. "I'm gonna have another drink. You ready?"

Cord declined with a shake of his head. "I can't carry you to bed tonight, Hank. They tell me I've got a bad back."

With a chuckle Hank slapped Cord's shoulder as he walked around the chair. "Is that what they say? Damned doctors, what do they know? You're a rock, O'Brien. A rock, steady as they come.''

''A rock with a crack in it,'' Cord mumbled into his glass.

''But it's working good, boy.'' Behind him Cord heard a clink and a splash, then the spinning of the cap on the bottle. ''You've got her fussing over you, and that's a good sign. Janet fusses over me, too. Althea never did. She'd never have slept in that trailer, not if her life depended on it. She lived in town while I built this house.'' Still steady on his feet, Hank rounded Cord's chair again, gesturing with his glass while he eased himself back down in the opposite chair. ''I suggested a trailer, too, thinking we'd build our home together, but she wouldn't have any part of it. She had to be close to an airport.'' He lifted an eyebrow. ''Jet-setter, you know.''

''How did a jet-setter ever get hooked up with you?'' It was an obvious question, but Cord wasn't sure he wanted to hear the story. He knew he wasn't going to like it.

''She had some friends in Texas, and I had some friends in Texas. I was starting out, had a few horses, thought I should hobnob with the big-time breeders. We met at a barbecue.'' He shrugged, studying his glass again. ''Maybe she was going through a stage or something. Maybe she was bored with the polo types and had a yen for a cowboy.''

Cord pictured Hank as he must have looked thirty years before—slimmer, harder, with a cocky look and an eye for the ladies. ''Seems like she could have satisfied a yen without getting married.''

Hank smiled, remembering. ''Oh, she was a fine lady, O'Brien. She was just as beautiful as Brenna is, just as fine. I don't know if she ever loved me, but she sure as hell enjoyed my company.'' He winked at Cord as he lifted his glass. "I made sure of that. Whenever we were together we had a good time."

"What happened?" Cord asked.

"She got pregnant. She didn't seem to mind too much at first, but then it started cramping her style. She stayed home—stayed *here* after she started showing, and even for a while after Brenna was born. But she was unhappy. She started taking trips back east again, taking the baby with her and staying longer each time. Pretty soon we were separated. It wasn't a decision anybody made. It just became a fact."

"Why didn't she divorce you?"

"I think she found it convenient to be married. Estranged, I guess you'd call it. The land was hers. She kept Brenna with her. She held all the cards. And then Janet came along." He sighed deeply and fortified himself with more whiskey. "Janet was a godsend—a woman who took my love and gave me hers. It was as simple as that. I told Althea there was someone else. I said, 'You can't expect me to live like a monk, woman.' She still wasn't interested in a divorce, and she wouldn't let me see my daughter. And that's the way things stood. I told myself I'd buy the land, I'd move, I'd go to Reno and get a divorce, but I never did. And I never crossed her over Brenna. No divorce, no custody battle." He lifted a sagging shoulder. "I'd have lost anyway."

"How did you know Brenna was even alive?"

"I kept in touch with Althea. She convinced me that Brenna was just as busy as she was, and I assumed Althea was raising a copy of herself." Grinning, he shook his head at his own mistake. "I sure was surprised when I started reading about Brenna in the horse journals."

Both men sat quietly for a long time, immersed in their own thoughts. There was the mother, and here was the daughter. Hank remembered a barbecue long past, a woman who laughed readily and danced as though she'd studied nothing else. Cord's memories were of a barbecue, too, and of a woman whose smile warmed his heart, a woman who danced with studied effort, afraid of making a mistake.

"What's this contest all about, Hank?" Cord finally asked.

"I don't know. A fool's notion, maybe."

Through narrowed eyes Cord studied the man. "I think she'll beat you."

"I think she'll stay around long enough to give it a try."

Cord nodded, then drained his glass. It made him shiver. He only used whiskey for medicinal purposes. *Therapeutic* purposes, he told himself, smiling lopsidedly at his glass. "I want to take Brenna away for a while."

"Away where?" her father demanded.

"Up to my place, if she'll go. Valiant can use some high-country training, and so can Brenna."

Hank took a minute to mull over the proposal. He knew what it meant. He hoped O'Brien knew what a chance he was taking, and he hoped O'Brien would take the chance. "Do you love her, Cord?"

Cord smiled. Hank never called him by his given name. "Sure feels like it."

"She's not like her mother. Anybody can see that. But still, she might not be able to live in your world."

"She might not."

"You're willing to risk it?"

"Don't see that I've got much choice, Hank. Comes a time when a man's gotta listen to the music."

Chapter Seven

When Cord suggested a trip to his Rocky Mountain home Brenna wanted to be persuaded. She'd thought about going back home—thought about it with no enthusiasm for the idea. It was the trial, she decided. The prospect of winning that endurance trial was her only reason for staying, and Cord offered her an opportunity to build another edge into her chances. He also offered her a way to put some distance between herself and Henry Sinclair without actually throwing in any towels.

Cord couldn't leave without taking care of his business first, and his business was shoeing horses. Brenna and Kyle had agreed to help him. Each was obviously surprised when the other showed up at the barn for a shoeing lesson, but they both pitched in and got the job done. They became an efficient team and, as time at the forge passed, a congenial one. Cord shaped shoes and hooves and, sitting straight-backed on a low stool, directed the nails, which Kyle and

Brenna took turns driving into the thickest part of the hoof wall. What had begun as a project to help Cord became a learning experience for both of them.

Brenna watched and listened, but Cord's intuitive "feel" for what was right wasn't something he could impart. He looked, judged, shaped and touched. A shoe that was off even a fraction of an inch could throw the angle of a horse's front legs off and cause soreness. Cord had a gift. In his hands shoeing became an art.

"I've been trying your method on Jack Daniels," Kyle confided to Brenna as she brought him more nails.

She frowned. "Jack Daniels?"

"What, you're sipping through a straw now instead of down the hatch?" Cord teased as he watched the two of them, bent over a big chestnut's upraised foreleg. They looked like a pair of male and female bookends, as much like full brother and sister as any he'd seen. They were Hank's kids, and they ought to have each other, he thought, even if Brenna never forgave Hank.

"Jack Daniels the *horse*. That big black gelding of mine." Kyle looked up at Brenna. "You've seen him, haven't you?"

Brenna nodded. "How's he coming?"

"I'm not sure I know what I'm doing, but his recovery time seems to be improving."

"That's what you want," Brenna said, glancing over Kyle's bent head at Cord. She saw approval in his dark eyes. "You've got a stethoscope?"

Kyle nodded. "I bought one."

"Keep it handy," Brenna instructed. "Listen to his heart and keep him below seventy-two, building his time. Don't let him get hot. A hot horse wastes energy."

"The Sheik does that," Kyle noted, glad his dad wasn't around to hear him.

"I know. I have to admit, the only horse I know that *never* does that—" she raised a brow Cord's way "—is Freedom. He never wastes anything. When I tell him 'that's it' he drops his head and turns into a plug."

"You question the wisdom of that?" Cord asked, grinning.

"I just hope nobody utters those words around him before the race is over."

"I won't if you won't," he vowed.

"When I cross the finish line I'll be well out of your earshot." Kyle looked up, and she turned her saucy grin on him. "Yours, too."

Cord laughed, laying a hand on Kyle's shoulder. "This lady sure knows how to set a man's jaw, doesn't she?"

She knew how to soften a man's heart, too, even while she hardened his...determination. In the dark Cord heard only the sound of her quiet breathing, even though the laboring of the pickup's engine as it hauled the horse trailer up another steep grade threatened to drown her out. She'd fallen asleep on the seat beside him, but he'd managed to maneuver her head onto his lap with very little sleepy objection. He wasn't so sure now that it had been a wise move. He hadn't imagined that she would turn out to be such a good snuggler.

He was glad they were almost home. Even with the specially designed cushion he'd gotten from the chiropractor, his back was killing him. Brenna had driven the first leg of the trip, the straight highway through the grasslands, but he'd taken the wheel through the Bighorns and beyond. It had been a long day. He smiled, remembering how close she'd had to move the bench seat to the dash in order to reach the clutch. She'd admitted that it had been a long time since she'd driven a standard shift, but she knew she could do it, and after stalling a couple of times she had gotten the hang of it. He wondered whether Althea would have made the effort. He also wondered how much of Althea had gone into the making of Brenna Sinclair.

He parked the pickup, squeezed her shoulder gently and whispered her name. She awoke slowly, turning the side of her face into his lap and muttering indistinctly. Cord dropped his head back and shifted his hips slightly, adjusting. God! what a feeling.

"Got a kiss for a very tired man?"

His voice drifted over her in the dark like warm water added to a cooling tub. The pickup wasn't moving, but his hand was, up and down her bare arm. She sighed her contentment. "Got a bed for a tired lady?"

"Have I got a bed for you." Conviction was in every word. "Two acres of sheets, nine down-filled pillows, a mattress that rivals the clouds—"

She sat up and found his face close to hers. "Mmmm."

"And a quilt made up of all the parts—" his lips brushed her forehead, mustache sweeping just behind "—of my naturally warm body."

"I'll take the bed," she murmured, returning his easy kiss. "You keep the quilt."

"It'll be close by when you need it," he whispered into her mouth before covering it with his own. The deep kiss sent Brenna into a soft, groggy haze. Then the porch light brought their heads around, and they sat there like two guilty teenagers, blinking at the man who stood on the porch of the small log house in front of them.

"I can unload the horses while you two get settled in," Jesse offered. "'Spoze you're both beat. Got some stew on the stove."

"Jesse's always got stew on the stove." The information

came out of the side of Cord's mouth, casting a shadow over the prospect.

"What's in it?" Brenna asked.

"You never know."

"*You* never care." Jesse opened the door and ushered Brenna inside. "It's a nice beef stew," he told Brenna. "Specialty of mine, and this boy eats it by the five-quart-pail." Then he noticed Cord's stiffness as he negotiated the steps. "How's the back?"

"Mine's okay." Cord dropped a genial hand on Jesse's shoulder. "How's yours?"

"Old. You two have something to eat while I unload your broomtails."

Brenna was hungry, and she had found that nothing satisfied her appetite lately better than one of the hearty stews people out West seemed to favor. It had never been one of her staples. She did miss seafood and fixed her sights on trout, but Jesse's stew was worthy of a request for seconds.

While Cord and Brenna discussed the pros and cons of various sleeping arrangements Jesse faded back into the woodwork. He knew he was sleeping in his own room. Those two kids could fight it out for the bed in Cord's room, which Jesse imagined to be comparable with President Lincoln's, and the day bed in the den. Cord would never be able to sleep in that little day bed, but such was his gallant proposal. Brenna would win the argument, of course, and lose the big bed, but Jesse figured it was just a matter of time before they shared it. In the end this whole thing might be a heartbreaker for one or both of them, but they were bound to share the bed. That much was fated.

The house was certainly adequate for two men's needs, Brenna decided, but she could think of a few small changes that would improve the decor. It needed a color scheme, for one thing. The living room had a lovely stone fireplace and varnished pine log walls, but the sofa and chairs were upholstered in tan and brown, and there were shapeless green curtains in the windows and a multi-colored braided rug on the hardwood floor. The lamps and end tables were functional odds and ends. The kitchen and dining room were well planned, with plenty of cupboards and counter space and a sliding glass door in the dining room, but again, a hodgepodge of colors had been used.

Cord's room was another matter. He explained that it had been added to the house on the other side of the living room wall. His stone fireplace stood back to back with the one in the living room. The poster bed was massive, and here there was a color scheme. Except for the varnished logs everything was cool blue, right down to the carpeting.

"Sure you don't want to change your mind?" he asked. "The view from that window is really something in the morning."

Brenna sat on the bed and bounced a couple of times. "This bed's pretty hard. Papa Bear must have a bad back."

Grinning, Cord sat next to her, hooking an arm over her shoulders for a friendly squeeze. "Nothing a little back rub wouldn't cure." He pulled her toward him and whispered in her ear, "Papa Bear doesn't mind sharing his bed with golden-haired little girls."

The flicker of his tongue against the curve of her ear made her shiver. She shrugged, murmuring, "If I see one, I'll send her in."

"I want one with red-gold hair and green eyes. No point in testing the bed in the den. You'll just say it's too soft." He nibbled at her earlobe.

"There's one other bed in the house," she reminded him.

"Yeah, but the troll sleeps there."

"What troll? There's no troll in this story." She giggled and squirmed when he nipped her.

"What story?"

"'The Three Bears.'"

"Three Bears?" His chuckle was lascivious enough for an adult bedtime story. "Ain't nobody here but Papa Bear and his old troll, little girl."

"I think I took a walk in the wrong woods."

"You're here now." He brought her head closer so he could give her the kind of kiss a man gives a woman who's sitting prettily on the edge of his bed, but she flinched just before his mouth touched hers. He drew back and saw that her eyes shimmered with fear. "But you don't want to be."

"I do," she said quickly. "I do want to be here."

"With me?"

"With you. But not..." He let his arm slide away from her as she stood. He made everything inside her liquefy, and she wanted two feet of space between them. "Cord, I'm no good at this. When people touch me, I...cringe."

"Not always," he said quietly.

She glanced up and then away, and he thought he saw something in her eyes that looked like guilt. "No, not...lately there have been times when..." Her eyes flew back to him, begging him to believe her. She didn't want to have to prove it to him. "I'm just no good at it, that's all."

"I am."

She took another step back as he rose slowly from the bed. "Good for you." She'd aimed for bravado, but her voice gave way to a rasp on the third word.

"Good for *you*," he corrected, smiling gently. "Are you a virgin, Brenna?"

"No." She gave her head a vigorous shake. "No, I took care of that a long time ago."

"How did you manage that?"

"The usual way, I suppose." Indignant now, she reminded herself that it had been an experience she hadn't cared to repeat.

"Cringing all the way?"

"No. *Yes*." There was desperation in her eyes, and it moved him. "Cord, I don't think you understand. The other night, I was…I was very…"

"I know." Reaching for her shoulders, he pulled her into his arms. "Relax," he whispered, running his hand up and down her back. "Not tonight, but soon, Brenna, I'll touch you until you forget how to cringe. I'll kiss you until you forget how to breathe, and I'll make love to you until you forget whatever it was you took care of the *usual* way."

"Cord…" Her insides were liquefying again.

"Not tonight, Brenna. But soon."

The first morning, when Brenna stepped out on the rustic veranda, the view took her breath away. The house and its outbuildings were set in a tree-lined meadow. Beyond that there were only mountains, so tall that they disappeared into the high-riding white clouds. The granite peaks were stippled with snow, and Brenna thought she could smell that snow-crispness when she took a deep breath.

It was Jesse who first showed Brenna the trails that wound among the spruce and pine. They varied from gentle slopes to steep climbs, always rocky, always challenging the horse and rider to pace themselves. The air was thin. Periodically they would top out for a wonderful view or break into an open meadow. It was an ideal training ground for endurance.

For four days Jesse took Brenna out for long rides. He refused to ride Freedom, so Brenna kept Valiant under her own strict tutelage in the morning and switched to Freedom in the afternoon. She realized that taking Freedom out after she'd worked Valiant was a pleasure. The Arab had to be coaxed a lot, but the mustang was home, and he seemed content to show Brenna around. Jesse, too, enjoyed the job of mountain guide.

The old man talked a great deal, and Brenna listened, becoming more at ease with him each day, until finally she was comfortable enough to wonder aloud, "What was Cord's mother like?"

As they had made their way downhill they had strung out, Brenna in the lead, and Jesse glanced at her back, considering the question for a moment. "She was slow to criticize and quick to laugh," he decided. "She could always make something good out of very little, whether it was a meal or a homemade bridle. And she was restless. Not so much at first, but after a while she'd get a look in her eye every so often, like she wanted to see what was on the other side of the mountain. Then she'd want to go into town for a few days, or she'd go up to Miles City or back to South Dakota. I could always tell she wanted to go because she always got that look in her eye."

"I think I've seen that look," Brenna said, remembering how tall the windows were in her mother's favorite restaurant and how green her mother's eyes had seemed when she was excited. "It usually meant Paris."

"You been to Paris?" Jesse wondered.

"Only once. I didn't see the attraction."

"Cord didn't either. He never wanted to go along. Took to these mountains like a duck to water. 'Course she saw that, same as I did." A cluck meant for his horse also punctuated Jesse's story. "Just as sure as she could never take to them, not permanent, anyways."

"Did she ask you to keep him?"

"No, not in so many words. She just stopped comin' back, and after a while we stopped lookin' for her."

"How long did it take before he stopped looking?"

Brenna had heard Jesse say "we," but she thought of Cord. She saw him sitting on the steps of the veranda, waiting.

"I don't know for sure, but I 'spect it wasn't too long. He knew her pretty well, and he didn't ask nothin' of her she couldn't give." After a pause Jesse added. "He don't ask that of any woman. I 'spect that's why he still ain't got one."

"You mean he doesn't trust them to stay around?"

"Don't think he's ever asked one to."

Brenna knew there was water ahead. The horses had smelled it before the sound of it became identifiable. Then she saw Cord's pickup, and her pulse rate increased. She took that as a sign that her workout in this thin mountain air needed to continue. But the view of the swiftly flowing mountain stream and the big man who wore waders and stood in it thigh-deep, casting his line into the water, told Brenna her pulse rate had little to do with the thin air.

"We're not far from the house," Jesse told her. "I'm goin' back and shine up the griddle. Looks like trout tonight."

Brenna let Freedom browse for grass while she sat on a weathered log and watched Cord reel his fish in. He was absorbed in the game, the fish bending the rod while he worked the reel. Finally the fish was out of the water, its rainbow stripe glinting in the evening sun's low-slung rays. Cord caught it in a net and carried it, squirming, toward the rocky bank. Seeing Brenna, he smiled and slogged a little faster.

The trout joined several others in Cord's ice chest. "You've had a good day," Brenna observed, peering into the chest.

"I'll be back in the saddle tomorrow," he declared with a note of triumph. "If I can cast, I can ride."

"How's your back?"

"Great." She'd been asking, but she hadn't offered any of her soothing ministrations in the last couple of days, and he wasn't going to push. She'd been enjoying herself, and that was what he wanted to see. Most women he knew enjoyed commotion—stores, restaurants, auditoriums, even grandstands and honky-tonks—but he'd always wondered whether there wasn't one somewhere who enjoyed getting closer to the sky. It might be Brenna, he thought, catching the smile she gave him. Brenna just might be the one.

Cord stowed the chest and his fishing gear in the back of the pickup before he greeted Freedom with a rub along his neck. "Think he'll take me back now, after he's fallen head over hocks in love with you?"

Brenna laughed. "It might take a little time. You'll have to talk nicely to him."

Cord threw his voice into a high pitch. "What would you like for din-din tonight, Freedom? Some nice hot oatmeal? With a little molasses, maybe?" The horse swung his head Cord's way, eyed him briefly, then lowered his muzzle to the ground with a disgusted snort. Brenna's laughter rolled on as Cord's voice dropped back to normal. "You're lucky the oats are even rolled, you ungrateful broomtail."

"Some horses prefer women," Brenna offered, shrugging. "I've seen it many times."

"Some horses prefer certain women, and this one's got his heart set on you." He leaned closer to Freedom's head. "If you throw that race for her, we'll be eating mustang meat around here instead of fish."

"Cord!"

Freedom grazed, unconcerned with human foolishness.

The flaky white fish was so delicious that Brenna didn't mind pulling an occasional bone from her mouth. She assumed that the men were less talkative than usual because they were doing the same. Jesse's pronouncement came after a long silence.

"I'm headin' into town for a few days. Anything you need?"

Brenna wasn't even sure how far "town" was, or what town he meant. She hadn't thought about towns for days. They had a radio, but no television, and the mail was delivered only three times a week to a box a couple of miles away. They had their own generator and battery system for electricity, and the well water was the sweetest she'd ever tasted. Brenna hadn't noticed that anything was missing. What could she need?

"Razor blades," Cord said, rubbing his jaw with one hand. "Indians aren't supposed to have much facial hair," he noted, apparently for Brenna's benefit. "My dad was white, though. Must've had one hell of a beard."

Without thinking Brenna reached across the corner of the table to touch his cheek. "I wouldn't say you have a heavy beard. And your mustache is soft."

Jesse lowered his nose into his coffee mug, but neither Brenna nor Cord noticed. They'd set up a magnetic field at their end of the table.

"Well, uh…it's Brenna's turn for dishes tonight anyway, so I thought I'd git along. Wanna hoist a couple beers yet tonight."

Brenna dropped her hand, feeling shaken. She tried to cover. "How far is it to…"

"Dubois," Cord filled in. "It's about forty miles. You should've left earlier, Jesse. Why don't you wait till morning?"

Jesse pushed his chair back and gathered his plate and utensils. "You got ears, boy. I got plans for tonight, and I ain't too old to carry 'em out. Anything else besides razor blades?'' He walked quickly to the sink, anxious to get going. These two were due for some privacy.

Nights were cool in the mountains and soft with dew. Brenna loved to stand on the veranda and listen to the night sounds—the harmony of chirps and croaks and the quiet overhead rustle of pine boughs. The screen door creaked open and clapped shut behind her, and she felt Cord's warmth at her back.

He took a deep breath and savored it. ''Ah, spruce boughs and pine pitch. Big improvement over the smell of fish.''

''Mmm, but that fish tasted so good, so fresh.''

''Better than your ocean fish?'' He put his hands on her shoulders and pulled her back against him, squeezing gently.

''At least as good as the best I've tasted,'' she assured him, letting her shoulders drop back.

''Do you like to fish?''

''I've never tried it. It looks like it might be fun to catch one, but I'm not sure I could throw the line out there.''

''I can show you how,'' he promised close to her ear. He slid his hand down her arm to her wrist and then put her through the motions of casting a rod. ''Draw it back slowly like this. Watch what you're doing, now. You don't want to get the hook hung up in something. Jesse once got it caught in his nose.''

''His nose! That's awful.''

''It was awful. I had to cut off the barb and unhook him. So you've gotta watch it.'' He nodded toward their hands and the imaginary rod over their shoulders. ''See that hook up there with one of my original lures and that little silver-colored weight?'' She looked. ''You see it, don't you?'' Brenna nodded. ''Okay, we're going to toss it way out there toward those trees. Smooth and easy, just a little flick of the wrist. Ready?''

"It's going to hit the porch roof."

"It's going to pass right through the roof," he promised, "and it'll land way out there. Okay, on three. Ready?"

Brenna glanced up, smiling, teasing. "*One* two three, *one* two three…''

"Let me do the counting, honey. This is my class. Ready?" He counted and guided her hand in an arc. Brenna could have sworn she heard a soft plunk in the water.

"I think I could do it," she mused, peering into the darkness for her imaginary line.

Cord turned her in his arms and laid one hand along her cheek, curving his fingers behind her head. The light from the window fell softly on her face, and he saw that peculiar combination of diffidence and desire that seemed to war within her. "I think you can, too."

"You wouldn't laugh at me if I messed up, would you?"

Her eyes were wide, trusting him to be honest. They spoke of more than fishing now. He shook his head. "I'd never laugh at you. Only with you."

"You laughed when I fell off the fence."

"You enjoyed that moment, and I enjoyed it with you. That was the first time I thought it might be possible for us to enjoy something together—the girl from the seaside and the guy from the mountains."

She lowered her eyes. "You mean the girl with the silver spoon in her mouth. The boss's brat."

He chuckled. "I stopped thinking of you that way long ago—starting that night, I guess."

Still she kept her eyes from him, and he waited, watching her pass the tip of her tongue over her lower lip before she spoke again. "And if I…didn't catch anything, would you be disappointed in me then?"

She had a way of reaching his heart. "You've caught something already, Brenna," he said quietly, tipping her chin up with his thumb. "Without even dropping a line."

His kiss was a prelude, and she knew it. He played on her lips with his until her mouth fell open and he dipped his tongue inside. Of their own accord her arms went around his shoulders and behind his neck as she returned his kiss, measure for measure. Uncounted moments later he moved his mouth away, and she managed to whisper, "I think you have all the lines, Mr. O'Brien."

"No, I'm not good with words," he protested. "Never been any good at..." His mouth came hungering after hers again, and she nourished him. He picked her up and held her several inches off the floor, taking everything her mouth had to offer. His brain pounded with it, and her head spun. They kissed until they remembered the need to breathe, and they came away gasping.

"Come inside with me, Brenna."

She closed her eyes and nodded, and he let her toes touch the floor again. He felt a quiver shimmy through her when he gathered her under his arm. He wished he had the right line for her, the one that would give her the assurance she needed. He took her inside, and when he reached the bedroom door he had a quick debate with himself about the advisability of turning on the light. His chuckle drew Brenna's frown.

"I guess I could use a good line right about now."

"I can do without one," she said. "You're taking me to bed; that's obvious."

He pulled his arm back and looked at her. "Half a minute ago it was obvious where *we* were going, Brenna— together. You cool off quickly."

"No, I don't," she insisted, clenching her fists at her sides. She hadn't cooled, and that was the problem. People always turned away. She'd learned to beat them to the punch, but at the moment she couldn't quite remember how it was done. "I don't. You have no idea how I feel. You have no idea what's inside me."

He saw the flash of anger and wondered who it was for. Certainly not him. He took her face in his hands. "Show me, then."

"No."

The anger was better than the fear. Fear was cold, but anger was hot. In the heat of her anger she would show him whatever it was she was afraid for him to see. "I'll make you show me."

"You can't." It was a brave retort, and she squared her shoulders with it. "No matter how strong you are, you can't—"

He kissed her, not to show her how strong he was, but because it was the first step. Her resistance was short-lived. It became another two-way kiss, demanding and responsive. No matter who was stronger, there was no weakness in the wanting on either side. He drew her to the bed, and she went willingly. She held him and kissed him willingly, but when he began undressing her, she panicked and pushed his hands away.

"No!" she gasped, tearing her mouth away. But her blood was on fire, and she needed him, and she didn't want him to go away from her now. She knelt on the bed, reached for his face, and pulled him back to her. "Just kiss me," she whispered. "Kiss me and then..." In the dim light she found his belt and tugged at it, her hands trembling with desperation.

Cord caught her wrists. She looked up at him, and he saw her confusion. He'd worked with too many wild horses to miss the obvious now. He didn't know whether she had lied about her virginity, but he figured it didn't matter. She might have had sex, but she'd never made love, not really. And she was afraid to.

"Don't stop." Her voice was a small delicate thing, pleading for tenderness. He laid her back on the bed.

"I'm not going to, not unless you've changed your mind."

"No," she said, almost too quickly. "I haven't."

"You aren't—" he settled over her and slipped one button free on her blouse "—protected, are you Brenna?"

"Protected? I...guess I should be." As though a hand over her blouse would do the trick, she clapped hers there.

"You will be," he promised, his voice husky as he closed his hand over hers. "Will you trust me to take care of it?" She nodded and let him carry her hand away. "I want to show you something, Brenna, but you have to trust me."

Her blouse was unbuttoned now, and she glanced away with a nervous smile. "I think you want me to show *you* something."

"It's not like that," he whispered, finding the fastener between her breasts. "You know that isn't what's going on with us."

"Oh, Cord, I know you're a good man." Her sigh was shaky. "I know that. I'm just..."

"You're a good woman." He dropped a soft kiss between her breasts and knew she shivered with it. "You're beautiful, Brenna. That's the first thing I noticed."

The hand that had clutched at her blouse now clutched the bedspread. She felt his mustache skitter across her breast, and her whole chest tightened.

"You make me feel good," he continued, letting his lips brush the words over her. "You make me laugh. You make me think. You make my pain go away." Feather-soft, feather-light, his lips teased her nipple. "You make my mouth go dry when I look at you," he whispered.

He touched her belly as he unzipped her slacks, and Brenna didn't breathe. Her breasts ached, and he only touched, only teased. When at last he took one small peak into his mouth, she groaned and gave herself up to the flickerings of his tongue. This was something she wanted; this was something that must never stop. With the utterance of his name, she told him so.

He could bridge her pelvis with his hand. God, she was small! Would he hurt her when he took her? Would he be too heavy for her? And would she, in this tiny cradle of hers, be able to carry his child? Not now, he reminded himself. Not now. But if she would stay…

His hand slipped lower, and he heard the sharp intake of her breath as she stiffened again. He took the protest from her lips with a kiss and found the source of her need with his hand.

Her pulse raced, and it seemed as though her temperature soared. Why did he…how could he… "Cord?" Oh, God. "Cord!"

"It's all right, baby. Show me how you feel. I want to know."

She felt like a shooting star. She felt like a firecracker. She cried out and came apart at the seams.

"Oh, Cord!"

"That's right, show me. Show me…."

Chapter Eight

The light from the living room spilled over the bed and filled Brenna's outstretched hand. It struck her that the familiar-looking hand might belong to someone else. She was shaken. She hardly knew herself, but the man who hovered above her obviously knew her well. She turned her face to him slowly, her breathing quick and shallow, her eyes full of wonder. Cord had given her a gift.

She put her hand to his face, smoothing her thumb over his mustache. He caught it in his teeth and slid his tongue over it. "You're trembling, too," she whispered.

He nodded, releasing her thumb with a parting nip and a kiss. "I'm scared."

"How could you be?"

"How could I *not* be?" He glanced down at the breast he'd laid bare and the concave belly that rose and fell between jutting pelvic bones so small, so delicate, that he hardly believed them human. "I need you now, and you might turn away from me."

"I…I wouldn't."

"When I held you in my hand, I thought…so small."

"I won't turn away."

"I'm a big man, Brenna."

She swallowed and swept the curling hair back from his temple. "You're the one who's beautiful," she breathed. "I noticed that right away, too. But I've been too dumb to notice how good you make me feel."

"I haven't even begun to make you feel good." But he had begun to take off his clothes, and he swung away to make quick work of it. Brenna shivered with the chill of his absence and wondered whether she should take hers off, too. He was sitting beside her before she'd decided, pulling her into his arms as he slipped her blouse off her shoulders and then helped her with her slacks.

He kissed her, gently to show her how he felt, then harder, to show her how it was with him. Brenna reached up and caught his head in her arms, tucking herself tighter into the pocket his body made for her. But he broke off the kiss and eased her away so he could see all of her. Watching him, she knew instinctively that she would like seeing herself through his eyes. His gaze lingered a little on each part of her, exempting nothing, enjoying the curve of her shoulder as much as the slope of her breast. Next time she looked in the mirror she would remember how he had looked at her. Next time there would be no childlike voice in the back of her mind suggesting flaws.

Cord ran his hand down her thigh and then drew it back quickly. His hand was too massive, too rough. He hadn't imagined the delicacy he would find beneath her clothes. He hadn't envisioned such refined skin, hadn't known that elegance could coincide with nakedness. Good God, he was a farrier; he made his living at the forge. His days were made of calluses and sweat, and his nights, when he wanted nights, were made of garish colors and loud music. His women had been gum-snappers, back-slappers, hip-swingers. What was he thinking, putting his hands on some-one like this, touching sandpaper to satin?

Brenna knew who he was. A line from a poem echoed in her head: "Under the spreading chestnut tree, the village smithy stands." She saw him in the bedroom shadows and in the shade of the towering tree, his arms as thick and brown as its branches. The hand that had quickened her body hovered tentatively over her thigh. His eyes shone, savoring everything they saw, but his hand was unsteady. Brenna took Cord's hand to her mouth and kissed his palm. Twice she kissed the hardened pad at the base of his little finger. "Touch me more."

Growling deep in his throat, he turned, laid her back against his pillow and braced himself over her. His head dropped so that he could touch her more, first with his lips, then with his tongue. There *was* a softness in him; she should have that first.

He brushed her with the fleece of his mustache, and his heart thumped within his ribs.

Her skin tightened over her body like the head of a drum.

He breathed the air his body had warmed over her breast, and his pulse pattered inside his head. He trailed the mois-ture from his mouth along a path of personal places, parts of her that responded to his selection with joyful shivers, while his loins throbbed.

Her senses sang his name as he buried his face in her neck, fighting for control.

Her need was stretched taut, and she offered it to him.

He answered with a thrust that knew nothing of softness.

* * *

Morning glories ran riot over the pine rail fence. They opened purple mouths to drink the morning mist and smile at the new-risen sun. Pine trees marched row on row toward the neighboring peak, green fading to misty blue against a granite and snow backdrop. The tall grass was wet with dew, and here and there a bit of yellow or white winked in the sunlight. Wildflowers or weeds, depending upon one's viewpoint. Brenna saw morning's glory, felt it down to her toes.

"You look cute in my clothes." Brenna turned, pulling Cord's shirt closed in front and holding it between her breasts. His hair was tousled, dipping over his forehead, and his smile was full of mischief. He swung his legs off the bed and sauntered to the window, a morning glory in his own right. "But you leave me nothing to wear."

"Surely you've got something in the closet."

"Nope. Everything's in the laundry." He hooked his hand behind her neck and pulled her close enough for a kiss. "How do you like the view?"

She raised one eyebrow and did a passable Mae West. "I'm impressed."

"There are other names for it, but I call it O'Brien's Peak," he told her, his eyes glinting.

"Clever. Whatever you lack in imagination, big boy, I'm sure you make up for in modesty." With an appreciative smile she returned a quick but affectionate kiss.

"Oh, Lord, it's hard to be humble…" he crowed off-key. Then he favored her with a cocky wink, adding, "When you feel so damn good in the morning."

Taking Cord's hand, Brenna flashed him a smile that said she took the credit for that and knelt, pulling him to the floor with her. They continued to stare out the huge bedroom window, which stretched from the beamed ceiling almost to the floor. "Look," she whispered, as though something might be startled by her voice. Cord's eyes followed her finger. Just outside a purple wildflower grew on a straight, dusty green stalk. Backlit by the morning sun, the petals were translucent, lavender with deep purple veins—tiny puffs of stained glass.

"It looks like a tiny blue heron," Brenna whispered, indicating the top bud, with its beaked petals, and the two wing-shaped buds below that.

"It does."

"And look," she said, her voice hushed with childlike wonder. Woven among tall blades of grass, a spider's web glittered with dew. Nearby the spider was busy weaving another web, one concentric hexagon outside the last. "She must need a guest room," Brenna speculated. She was so engrossed that she hardly noticed she'd been pulled into Cord's lap.

"She can use mine." He touched his lips to her temple and came away with a wisp of her hair trapped in his mustache. He laughed, and it fell away.

"I'm staying in the guest room," Brenna reminded him. "I suppose you think you've made some sort of conquest."

He lifted her chin in his hand and waited until she allowed herself to look up at him. "I think *you've* made some sort of conquest—over something you must have been fighting with for a long time. Last night you stopped fighting. You let me touch you."

Blinking rapidly, she took a deep breath. "I told you the truth about my...I wasn't..."

"I don't care what you weren't," he said, his eyes tugging gently at her soul. "You *were* untouched. You've never let anyone get that close to you before. Why is that, Brenna?"

"No one's ever wanted to." It was the truth, as she knew

it. She hadn't been inaccessible, not entirely. She'd assumed that no one had supposed her to be worth the effort.

He raised a brow. "That's hard to believe."

"No one's ever tried very hard," she amended.

"You mean your resistance has always outlasted anyone else's efforts. No wonder you and Freedom get along so well."

The mention of Freedom gave her the chance to jump the fence to more comfortable ground. "You're getting along with him better now, too."

Tracing the line of her cheek with his forefinger, he thought how dewy she looked in the early-morning light, how soft and satisfied. "I've taken your advice seriously," he told her. "I've been talking to him, telling him that what I want him to do is something men and horses do naturally together. Remember that sermon you gave me?"

There was nothing delicate about his hands, she thought. She didn't think she'd ever known a man with callused hands, not this way. But then, whose hands had she known this way? Whose hands had known her this intimately?

How could hands with hardened skin be so sensitive? she wondered. How could they tell when a horse's hoof was just a fraction of an inch off the proper mark? He turned the back of his hand to her cheek and moved it slowly, making her believe that even the fine down on her face had nerve endings. How could work-hardened hands be so sentient, ferreting out a responsiveness she'd never known she had? His hand slipped down to the side of her neck and then to the ridge of her collarbone, and, yes, she wanted him to touch her. Risky, too risky. She might end up wanting to be with him, and he might prefer his independence. A little touching could be a dangerous thing.

"When will we be going back to Pheasant Run?" she asked.

"Whenever you think you've had enough." Her eyes flashed, and he smiled, moving his shirt back from her breast. "Mountain air. Some people find it too stimulating."

"Maybe that's what it is." When his hand covered her breast she froze, mid-breath. In view of the risks she'd had it in her mind to call a halt. "Cord..."

"Brenna, this is what men and women do together naturally." Leaning down, he let his lips follow the path his hand had taken along her neck, whispering to her between open-winged butterfly kisses. "Look how naturally you're sitting on my lap."

Her bottom was as bare as his legs were, and, had he pointed that out to her a few minutes before, she might have pulled away. Not that she hadn't been feeling the heat between them, but pretending she didn't feel it made it permissible. Now, as his mouth touched her breast, the very concepts that went with *pretending* and *permissible* were extinguished from her mind. She dropped her head back and filled her lungs with the scent of him.

"You tell me that and then—" she felt his tongue and could only whisper the last "—you take my breath away."

Her head touched the carpet first as he lowered her to the floor, promising, "I won't take anything from you, Brenna, not your spirit or your freedom. I just want to give you what I gave you last night."

"But, Cord, we're right by the window."

"There's only the spider, and she won't tell."

His kiss cut off any further protests, and his hands made her forget what they were. He took nothing but the capacity to speak and think coherently. Small powers of limited importance. She could feel. He gave her the most excruciating tingling, the most indelicate surge of moisture, the most impossibly deep tension. Yes, by heaven, she could feel, and what she felt was Cord O'Brien. He filled every sense she had.

"Cord, I can't...I can't stand it—please! Help me."

The desperate plea brought his head up. Her green eyes looked teary, and that unnerved him. Was it fear? Did she dread his penetration even as she begged for release? Had he hurt her the night before? "Brenna, I can stop." Her hands tightened at his waist, and there was a wildness in her eyes. "There are other ways..."

"Please! I want you everywhere. I want to be filled with...you."

He tried to go easy, but she would have none of that. She lifted her hips to him, dug her nails into his buttocks, and drove him to the brink of madness with the soft moaning sound she made deep in her throat. He lost himself in her, but she found him, wrapped him in her passion, and reveled in every ounce of magic that was Cord.

Utterly spent and drifting in the euphoria they'd conjured together, they lay by the tall window and watched the lazy dissipation of the morning mist. Sunshine brought new colors to the soaring pines and the meadow that was Cord's backyard. Emeralds and brown greens gave way to sunlit yellow greens, with the spruce-blue shadows lurking distantly where the timber became denser on the slopes. It all looked different, Brenna thought. Today she saw every shade, every gradation of every needle, each shifting glint of the sun.

"I never met a tall window I didn't despise," Brenna mused. "Until this one. This one is lovely."

Propping his head on his elbow, Cord inspected the window, ceiling to floor. "I can't imagine despising a window unless it was too small."

"My mother used to take me to a restaurant that had very tall windows. Tall and narrow. I hated going there."

She sounded distant. That scared him, because he wanted to keep her close. She'd come so far in such a short time, and he wasn't sure he wanted to know where or what she'd come from. He just knew he didn't want her to go back there. He pulled her back against him, fitting her to him like one spoon inside another so they could both look out the window. Touching his cheek to her hair, he willed her to see the beauty through this window and forget those she'd despised in the past.

"We'd sit by the window, and she'd tell me her plans for summer or for Christmas," Brenna continued. Strangely, these memories were ready to come out. The window was wide as well as tall, the expansive view inviting openness, and the shoulders behind hers were broad.

"She'd tell me where she could be reached if I needed anything. Unless it was an emergency, the housekeeper could probably take care of it, she'd say. By the time she decided I was presentable enough to take along, it was too late. I hated the restaurant and the tall, narrow windows, and I hated her. Paris, for all its treasures, turned out to be a great disappointment. It came much, much too late.

"I wanted to punish her for that, and I promised myself that if she ever did try to touch me, I would turn away. But she never did." His hand felt wonderful on her shoulder, and she dropped her head back to his chest to let him know, adding hastily, "That was fine with me. I had my horses by then. I began training them when I was in college. I leased several stalls right on campus and had a waiting list of clients by the time I graduated. I had no more time for Althea than she had for me, and we both knew that."

"You never tried to contact your father?" he wondered, gentling his voice. "Not once in all those years?"

"No. I saw no point in it. My mother made it clear that the ties had been severed and that he had a new family, a fact that she found distasteful, but not surprising. He was, in her words, a 'common man' behaving in a very 'common' way." And then her mental window on the past widened to include Cord's memories. "Did you? Did you ever try to find your father?"

"No." But I had Jesse, he thought. Another "common" man.

"I don't think people should throw each other away." It wasn't a bid for anything. It was simply a belief she'd held too dear to share with anyone until now. "Do you?"

It took him a moment to find his voice. "No, I don't."

"So you can't let them get you. Not even small pieces of you that they might consider inconsequential and toss aside. Do you know what I mean?"

"Yes. I know." Could she really believe such a thing was possible? Giving was part of her nature; didn't she realize that? No matter how hard she'd tried to keep her heart under lock and key, it had escaped, and the wonder of it was that he held this fragile treasure in his big, rough-hewn hand. "Remember when you rubbed my back, Brenna?"

That rich, husky timbre near her ear made her shiver inside as she thought of putting her hands on him, smoothing them over his skin without reserve. "Yes."

"You took a piece of me then. Did you know that?" She shook her head. "You took my pain," he explained. "What did you do with it?"

"I...I don't know."

"I think you kept it. You took it, and you couldn't throw it away, so you kept it. I know how hard it was for you to do that, and I'm going to do the same for you sometime when you're hurting." The promise was made with a kiss on the curve of her ear. "Remember that, and don't be selfish with it when the time comes."

Brenna turned to him, settling on her back and smiling up at him. "I can't imagine where I could be storing your bad back, Mr. O'Brien, but if I start feeling any twinges you'll be the first to know. Right now I'm in remarkably good health."

He gave her a crooked smile, his mustache twitching as he raised one dark eyebrow. "You look *flushed* with good health, Miss Sinclair."

"Mountain air." Then she remembered something and frowned. "Why were you going to stop?"

He remembered, too, and his stomach tightened. "I thought you looked scared. I thought maybe I'd hurt you before."

Her smile returned, and she shook her head. "You mean, you really would have stopped cold?"

"I would have tried." His chuckle rumbled in his chest. "I would have stopped hot and showered cold. I was damn glad you didn't put me to the test."

"Why not? You've passed every one so far. You could have played Superman if you hadn't had a—"

"Bad back," they chimed in unison. Laughing, he pulled her into his arms and rolled one full turn across the floor with her before he levered himself over her, grinning. "How's that for an invalid, huh? Wanna see how strong I am? Wanna see how many push-ups I can do?"

She looked up at his silly grin, at the black hair tumbling over his forehead, and she giggled, delighted. "That's for arms!"

"Four arms! What do I look like, an octopus?"

"From this angle you look like a gorilla in a tree. Maybe you should do chin-ups."

"That's what I want you to do—keep your chin up," he instructed, lowering himself slowly. "I get a kiss for each one. Deal?"

"Deal." And she gave him the first of many in a game Cord O'Brien could have kept up indefinitely. There was nothing wrong with his biceps.

Jesse hadn't lived this long without learning that there was indeed a time for every purpose under heaven. He'd apparently decided it was time to make himself scarce. Whenever Brenna asked Cord told her that Jesse would be along when he'd had all the fun he could stand for the summer. Privately Cord knew Jesse would give him a week or more with no questions asked, no explanations required. They'd talked about a time when they might build another house up here, but so far there'd been no need for that. They respected each other's needs for time and space alone. When Cord's time with Brenna had passed, Jesse would still be there.

Cord had considered the possibility that he and Jesse might be the only two human beings the Almighty had cut out for this particular spot on the mountain. The Mc-Culloughs lived about eight miles down the road, but they hardly counted as human beings; they'd started looking just as craggy as the face of the mountain they lived on, and they squawked like a couple of buzzards. The old Trent place was empty; the Trents had moved on two years ago, and no one had bought the house and land. The living wasn't easy here. It was isolated. It got lonely. This was unforgiving country, but Cord had never found its equal in beauty. When he was away from it he carried it with him, firmly embedded under his skin, and he counted the days until he would see it again.

It bothered him that he was beginning to think about Brenna the same way. He knew she cared about him, but he also knew that it was common for two people to come together and care about each other for a time before admitting to each other that there were other things that were more important. Thinking about who she was and what kind of world she'd come from was a sobering exercise. Then he would follow her through the pine woods on horseback, watch her break through to a sunlit meadow or a scenic overlook, glimpse the radiant glow on her face when she turned to see that he was right behind her, and he would get high all over again.

Their days were idyllic, spent doing chores, riding, walking together. Catching sight of an elk or a deer or even a rabbit had never become commonplace for Cord. In all the years he'd lived in the mountains, a glimpse of a free-roaming moose had never failed to stop him in his tracks. Now it would stop Brenna, too. She came to expect his sign—an upraised hand, a finger to his lips—and soon she stopped scaring everything away.

Twice they saw bands of sleek wild horses running free in the valley below their vantage point. The first time Freedom lifted his head, pricked his ears and trumpeted to them, but they galloped on. The second time they spotted the small herd Freedom let them pass without calling to them, but not without lifting his head and his heart in their direction. Brenna watched them dart into the trees and then looked Cord's way with a comment on the tip of her tongue, but his heart had tagged after them, too.

A black bear bounded across a meadow not fifty yards from where they stood on an upwind slope one morning, and Brenna, who spotted him first, nearly leaped out of her skin. Forgetting Cord's calm signals, she clapped one hand over her mouth and tugged on his arm with the other. The word "bear" was there in the wild look in her eyes. She managed to direct Cord's attention to her find before the animal got away.

"That was a bear!" she gasped.

"That was a bear," Cord agreed. "A black bear."

"I'll say he was black! And shiny. Did you see how glossy his coat was? Did you see how fast he moved?" She had both hands around his arm, and she squeezed for punctuation.

"I saw. He was beautiful."

"And big! Wasn't he big? What if he'd seen us?"

"He'd have kept right on going." When she got excited her eyes sparkled. Cord loved it. Touching him to share her excitement was something she did more often now, and when she put her hands on him, he got excited, too. "I'm the only bear in these woods who really likes golden-haired girls."

Evenings were spent in front of a chill-chasing fire, either in the living room or in Cord's bedroom. They would take their after-supper coffee to the hearth, pile pillows on the floor and talk. Cord had long been an avid reader. The cardboard boxes full of paperbacks that Brenna had found stashed under his bed and in every closet attested to his love for historical novels, particularly Westerns. The boxes also contained how-to books, mysteries, and a great deal of history. Cord's training after high school had been vocational, but his education had come in these boxes.

"Valiant and Freedom are working equally well now," Brenna told him one night. She lay on her stomach, elbows braced on a plump pillow, her bare feet hiked up in the air above her back. Her riding breeches ended at mid-calf, and she'd loosened the Velcro fasteners below her knees. Sitting beside her, arm hooked over one upraised knee, Cord resisted laying a hand on the small, round bottom that always tempted him. "Of course, Freedom's recovery time is still faster," Brenna admitted, "but Valiant makes better time on the flat."

"Valiant's legs are longer," he said absently, admiring her own short but shapely calves.

"He's bred for speed and conditioned for endurance. Perfect combination." Turning on her side, Brenna propped her head on an upraised arm and faced him. "Why raise mustangs, Cord? And why race them? Why not just let them run free?"

"Like the bands we've seen?" She nodded. "Most of those are just wild horses. The true mustangs are few in number, getting fewer all the time. If we don't breed them in captivity they'll be gone soon. And they're unique among horses. They've been around a long time—stuck it out through thick and thin." He tossed a nod over his shoulder toward the big window, where the high peaks loomed over darkening valleys. "There's a lot of thin up in the high country. I admire their staying power. The mustang is worth keeping around."

"If Freedom wins the Rocky Top race he'll be quite a valuable horse." She ran a contemplative finger around the rim of her coffee cup.

"He *is* a valuable horse. I just want to let that be known."

"By winning the race."

He nodded, lifting a shoulder in a shrug. "Yeah, that would help."

Raising her eyes to his, she offered an apologetic smile. "I'm not going to enjoy beating you, Cord. I do hope you come in second."

Cord laughed, loving her innocent sincerity. "Honey, I'm riding to win," he vowed, catching her chin in his hand. "But when I do, you remember how much work you've put into that bull-headed cayuse. You'll be a winner, too."

"I'll take his award for best conditioned, thank you."

"I'll take his trainer..." Stretching out beside her, Cord reached over her hip and filled his hand with the target it had been itching for all evening. She lifted her head for the kiss she knew was coming. She returned it, and he groaned and whispered into her mouth, "Thank you."

They had to go back sooner or later. Cord had a job waiting for him at Pheasant Run, and Brenna—well, Brenna was a visitor. She was Cord's guest in his home, Henry's guest at Pheasant Run. No matter who held the deed to the property, Brenna was a guest there. She thought about it on the drive back. She was losing the heart she'd guarded closely for years, and she was only a guest here. No matter how she felt about Henry Sinclair, she knew she couldn't turn his family out of their home. She would end up selling Pheasant Run to the man who'd given it his life's blood, and then she would go back to Connecticut. Cord O'Brien, she remembered, had never asked any woman to stay.

It was late when they arrived. Pheasant Run was asleep. After they'd unloaded the horses Brenna returned to her room at the house, and Cord went wearily back to the trailer. He shed his shirt, pulled off his boots and fell into bed. As he drifted off to sleep he thought that the bed felt good, but it would feel even better with Brenna's body next to his.

He slept long and hard. The pounding in the distance was at first just an irritation he ignored, but when he heard his name, he dragged himself to his feet.

"Cord! It's Brenna. Please wake up."

If the attempt at a loud whisper hadn't sounded so panicky it would have made him laugh. "I'm up. C'mon in."

The door opened, and she stuck her head in. The morning sun was low in the sky, and the interior of the trailer was shadowy. She stepped inside as he padded barefoot to the kitchen sink, turned on the cold water and splashed a handful over his face. Whatever he grumbled into his hand was probably best ignored.

"Something's wrong with Valiant," Brenna explained.

"He probably doesn't want to get up this early." It took another handful of water to wake Cord up. Poor horse probably needed a whole trough.

"He's lame."

"Front or back?" Cord demanded, pulling a towel over his face.

"Front," she reported. "Both front feet."

Cord looked up, concern registering in his face. "You changed his feed lately?"

"He was getting hotter feed while we were up at your place. He was working harder."

Cord found his boots under the table and his socks on the floor—the trail he'd left the night before. "More corn?"

"A little. I'm careful with corn."

"Could he have helped himself while you weren't looking?"

"I'm *careful* with hot feed, Cord. I know what it can do."

He heard her indignation and sympathized with it. But the best of intentions could be fouled up by someone who was too clever for his own good. "You didn't ride him this morning, did you?" he asked, stuffing his shirt into the waistband of his jeans.

"No. He's lame."

"Let's go find out why," he suggested, ushering her out the door.

The reason was obvious. As he stood in his stall Valiant leaned back on his hindquarters, favoring both front feet. Cord picked up each hoof and examined it, knowing full well that he would find the characteristic bulging in each sole. He stood slowly, brushing his hand on his thighs and looking Brenna in the eye.

"He's foundered."

Chapter Nine

The veterinarian approved of the cold water soaks Brenna
had begun on Valiant's front feet. He prescribed a pain
killer and told her that the rest would be up to her farrier,
adding, "You have the best."

After the vet had left Brenna stood back and let Cord do
his best. He went about it with little conversation and
hardly a glance her way. Jesse's remedy for founder, or
laminitis, as the scientists called it, was a bran poultice in
gunny sacks, which were tied over the inflamed feet. Valiant had already lain down when Cord applied the poultice.
Resting with his nose hanging over his forefeet, he was no
longer the proud, high-headed Arabian, the horse Brenna
had been convinced could scale Pike's Peak without getting
winded. His ears and his eyelids drooped, and he was rem-
iniscent of an old, gray pack mule.

Cord had never been sure where Jesse's remedies came
from, or whether they were documented in any journal of

veterinary medicine, but he knew they usually helped. Much of Cord's "best" was actually Jesse's. Cord had gone to school to become a farrier because Jesse had said there was a lot to be learned from books and schools, and he'd been right. Cord had studied beyond the basic training program. He'd never used the courses he took in animal science toward a degree, but he'd studied because he was interested in genetics and livestock management.

No matter how much he read or studied, he found that Jesse's common sense always rang true. With Jesse he'd learned by the seat of his pants and had come to know the right "feel" in his hands. He'd seen that after the vet had done all he could do, Jesse usually had one more remedy up his sleeve. Nine times out of ten Jesse did know best, and it was that experience, passed into Cord's hands and enhanced by Cord's training, that he brought to bear in treating Valiant. He owed Brenna that much.

She waited just out of reach, but he was aware of her with the periphery of his attention. Surely she'd seen founder before, but he doubted that she'd seen anyone tie gunny sacks over the animal's sore feet, and he expected her to question him on it. She didn't. She just stood there and watched. It had happened at his place, probably in his corral or his barn. Brenna never let a horse drink too much when he was hot, never put him up wet, never let him get chilled. Somehow Valiant had gotten into some high energy, or "hot," feed and had eaten like a horse. As he worked Cord racked his brain, trying to remember whether he had left anything out, or whether he'd found the barn door open when it shouldn't have been. He remembered nothing out of place, but somehow this had happened.

Properly treated, founder usually didn't keep a horse out of commission for more than a week. Hoof damage was the most common result, but, with special shoeing the animal could function normally in most cases. But Valiant was headed for the Rocky Top Endurance Race, one of the most grueling competitions of its kind. He had to be absolutely sound within a few weeks.

Cord uncoiled himself slowly and rose to his feet, brushing his hands off on the back of his jeans. Brenna watched him flex his shoulders and settle both hands at his waist, the better to knead the kinks out of his lower back. Standing just outside the stall, Brenna gripped the handle on the Dutch door. She had a terrible urge to go to him, to move his hands aside and massage his back herself. But he'd barely spoken to her as he'd worked. Did he think she'd been careless with the horse? Did he really imagine she didn't know what overfeeding could do to an animal?

Brenna was always careful. She was a person who never allowed herself to make mistakes. When she made them in spite of herself, she held herself in contempt for them and expected others to do the same. She was braced for it now. She would deal with Cord's scorn first. Sooner or later, she would face Henry Sinclair, too, and she would hold her head high, shouldering the blame, hiding the shame of whatever error she should have known better than to make. Cord turned to her. She read nothing in his face, but she flinched.

He saw condemnation in her eyes and knew it was for him. No matter what had gone wrong, all he could do was try to make it right. "I'll keep an eye on him today," he promised, closing the distance between them gradually. "I want to keep that mash on him for a while; it'll help take down the swelling. Then I'll shoe him."

"I'll stay with him. I'll make sure he doesn't tear into those bags and eat whatever's in them."

They stood with the half door between them, each blaming himself for what nobody had done. "I have some work to do on a couple of Hank's geldings," he told her. "I can cross-tie them right by this stall. Valiant won't move without me knowing about it." There was nothing soft in her face—not a crease, not a smudge, not a tear. She stared past him at the horse, and he wondered whether he dared touch her. "I'm sorry about this, Brenna," he offered quietly.

She glanced up at him, puzzled. *He* was sorry? Why? Because a good horse was down? "I am, too," she said, stiffening.

What was *that* supposed to mean? he wondered. The way she stood there with her nose pinned up so high made the words sound like a high-class kiss-off. "Look, I'll take care of it. I can't guarantee you a racehorse in three weeks, but you'll have a saddle horse."

"Henry will have a saddle horse," she reminded him. "And the deed to Pheasant Run."

"You've got more than that at stake." Cord caught her shoulders in his hands. "Open your eyes, Brenna."

"My reputation is at stake." She met his eyes with a level stare. "This project means a great deal to me. I've kept a journal; I've devoted time and effort..."

"Is that it?" He hadn't realized he was squeezing so hard until she grimaced and shrugged away. "Your reputation?"

"It's hard won. I was just told that you're the best at what you do; you know the value of a good reputation."

"And just how do you figure any of this affects your reputation? You don't *lose* a race when you can't enter."

"My horse foundered."

"So? Nobody knows that except—"

"*I* know it!" She tapped her finger in the center of her chest. "A trainer—a *good* trainer—does not let a horse founder. I was careless. I know it, and Henry Sinclair knows it...." Now her eyes went soft. Now there was a soft pucker around her mouth, and a slight crease in her brow. "And you know it, Cord. You know it, too."

Brenna took a step back as Cord moved from the stall, closing the door behind him. "I thought you blamed me."

"You? Of course not. Valiant is my responsibility."

"He was at my place."

"I've gone over it in my mind, everything we did the last few days, and I can't figure out when it happened."

"It doesn't matter." He lifted her chin in his hand, and she looked up. "I've thought about it, too, and I figure it was nobody's fault. I'm just sorry it happened."

"I am, too."

He smiled. "I guess we've established that. So while I do you a favor, I want you to do me one."

"What's that?"

"Work Freedom for me."

Though it wasn't a question, he waited for an answer. Brenna nodded, and a heaviness dissipated within her chest.

In the next few days Cord kept close track of Valiant's forefeet. Brenna watched and was satisfied that his reputation was indeed well deserved. With special shoes, a plastic sole and a cushion of silicone protecting the bottom of each tender foot, Valiant was soon able to walk without dragging his toes. Brenna worked at keeping him fit by exercising him on a longe line, moving him from a walk to a trot to an easy canter as his condition improved. But she knew she wouldn't race him. She hadn't said it yet, but she had settled it in her mind. Returning the curry comb to its bin and the big, bristled body brush to its shelf in the tack room, Brenna told herself that she was out of the race.

"Does she think she's going to ride that lame horse in the Rocky Top trial?"

Brenna's ears pricked at the sound of Henry Sinclair's

voice. He'd said nothing to her about Valiant's condition since they'd come back from Wyoming. He'd watched from a distance as Cord treated the horse, but he'd said nothing. Brenna wondered whether he was angry, or delighted with this turn of events. Neither emotion had shown on his face.

"She hasn't said," Cord's voice answered. The clomp and shuffle of mens' boots were accompanied by the clatter of a shod horse, probably one Cord was returning to the barn.

"What do you *think* she thinks she's going to do?"

Cord's quick laugh was a comment in itself. "If I thought I had to know, I guess I'd ask her."

"I'm not pushing, O'Brien. I told you, I'm not pushing."

"You're not talking to her, either."

"Don't know what to say." A stall was opened, and Brenna heard Cord cluck softly, heard the horse's hooves swish through the bedding straw. The stall door clicked shut. "What the hell can I say?"

"What would you say to Kyle?"

"I'd say, 'Tough luck, boy. You'll get 'em next year.'"

"Well?"

Silence. "Hell, I can't say that to Brenna. She won't be here next year."

"*You* might not be here next year."

Silence. "Well, she can't ride that lame horse, O'Brien. She might get her neck broken. You tell her that."

"You tell her that." Another stall door opened, but it was closed again almost immediately. "You can't say much of anything to her, can you, Hank? What are you afraid of? Have you told her you love her?"

Silence. "Have you?"

The silence grew heavy. "I didn't think you were a meddler, Hank."

"I wasn't. Didn't used to be, anyway. It's different with a daughter." The stall door opened again, and Brenna knew by the swishing straw that Cord had turned his back on Henry and entered the stall. "O'Brien—" the movement in the stall halted "—what are *you* afraid of?"

If there was to be an answer, Brenna didn't want to hear it. She slipped quietly from the tack room and into the open air, which she welcomed into her lungs with a deep breath. They'd been talking about her. *Her*, Brenna Sinclair, not some stuck-up Dresden doll. What would two full-grown men have to fear from her? There were questions of love, but no answers. Why weren't there any answers?

"Brenna?"

The voice was Kyle's. Brenna had walked briskly through a series of gates without any direction in mind. She'd simply wanted to put the stud barn behind her. Now she'd run into Kyle. He was leading the black gelding she'd seen him ride before. Remarkably, the horse was saddled with English tack.

"This must be Jack Daniels," Brenna guessed, summoning a smile in appreciation of Kyle's change in tack. "Are you giving the Sheik a break?"

"I've been working the Sheik pretty hard, but I have time for Jack, too. I was just taking him out. Wanna try him?"

The anxious look in Kyle's eyes was somehow alluring. Brenna stood back to give the gelding an appraisal. "He looks good, Kyle. Nice conformation. Good muscle tone."

"I've been keeping close watch on his vital signs, working him at the slow gaits like you said. He's doing real good. Wanna try him out?" The question was put to her almost urgently this time, and while Brenna hesitated, Kyle pressed the reins into her hand, adding, "Go ahead."

Jack Daniels had real promise, Brenna judged as she

paced him round and round the big ring. Kyle leaned over the top rail, grinning his approval as he watched. It struck Brenna that the boy really wanted to please her. The boy— her brother—wanted her to approve of the work he'd done.

"He's wonderful, Kyle. He's certainly one of the smoothest horses I've ever ridden."

"He's fast, too." Kyle took the reins she handed back to him, and the two of them walked together, Jack Daniels following close behind. "I was thinking maybe you'd enter him at Rocky Top…instead of Valiant, I mean."

Brenna squinted up at the boy, raising her hand to shade her face from the sun. Hope sprang like a fountain in his hazel eyes. "But I haven't trained him."

"You could take over right now—today. I've been doing just what you said, Brenna; it's just like you've been training him yourself. And you've got more than a week to finish him out."

Brenna looked back over her shoulder at the gelding and then back up at Kyle. "Even if I took over this minute I couldn't say I'd trained this horse. This is the horse *you* should be riding at Rocky Top."

"I have to ride the Sheik." Kyle glanced away, and Brenna didn't miss the wistful note in his voice. "It means a lot to Dad to run the Sheik in that race. It means a lot to Pheasant Run."

"You mean because of the bet?" she asked. The bet had become an afterthought in her desire to compete in the race. She'd used her methods to train a horse that had been considered a cull, and she knew she'd made a winner of him. She'd make him something worthy of Henry Sinclair's respect and admiration—something, like Cord's mustangs, worth keeping around.

"Because it would be good for the Sinclair Arabs." Kyle's shrug was boyish, as was the way he swept his sandy hair away from his forehead. "I think the bet is kinda silly. Who cares who owns the land? Pheasant Run *is* Hank Sinclair, and you're his kid, same as I am." He looked down at her again, his face full of innocence and honesty. "I want you to have a Sinclair Arab to ride in that race, Brenna. Jack Daniels is my best offer."

Brenna's eyes burned, but she managed a convincing smile. "I like your best offer very much, Kyle. And I appreciate the thought. I really do."

"But no dice, huh?"

Brenna shook her head. "I've never cared much about labels or brand names, but it would have been a good contest between Valiant and the Sheik."

"And you think you'd have had a sweet victory?"

"I'm afraid the dark horse would've had us both beat."

"You mean Freedom?"

Brenna raised an appreciative brow. "I mean Freedom."

The lilting strain of "Für Elise" traveled easily on evening's cooling air and teased Cord's mind. He'd skipped supper at the house, and now he lingered over the job of cleaning his tools, oiling all the nippers and tongs, honing all the cutting edges. Nails were organized in their compartment, rasps cleaned and lined up in theirs. Cord's hand moved mechanically from mallet to hoof tester, his head filled with music.

In his head he'd already gone into the house and taken a seat on the sofa, where he could see the side of her face, the soft underside of her chin, the movement of her hands. Her hands caressed the white keys and stroked the black ones, and they made music for her—blissful, romantic music. Once, when he'd ached so badly that he'd had to squeeze back tears whenever he tried to move, she had touched him that way. But she hadn't touched him that way since. She'd reached for him because he'd made her want him, but she hadn't felt free to touch him as though his body were an extension of hers, as though his ache were hers and his pleasure hers also. If she would touch him the way she touched those piano keys he would make music for her, too. Blissful, romantic music.

The big, wooden toolbox slammed shut under Cord's hand. He ached now, damn it, just as badly as he had when he'd lain flat on his face for an interminable length of time on a plywood mattress. Had he told her that he loved her? Hell, there wasn't any point in making declarations like that to a woman who'd just inherited half of Connecticut, or whatever state she was from, and a handsome piece of South Dakota as well. He'd shown her how he felt; she could take it or leave it. If she took it, she would have to take it in the mountains of Wyoming, and if she left it, she left it for good. He wasn't interested in any jet-setter. If they were rich, they were called jet-setters—poor, you called them tramps. Rich or poor, a restless woman left a man with a cold bed and a sick heart.

Cord watched the Western sky redden as the sun dropped toward the horizon. He hadn't been to town in—how long had it been? A couple of months? He could do with a few laughs and some foamy tap beer. Maybe a different brand of music would sound good for a change, too.

"I have absolutely no doubt that you can win that race. You are, without a doubt, the best looking specimen I've seen *ever*, and I don't say that just to flatter your ego. I know flattery will get me nowhere with you. No, I say it because it's true. I've never seen anyone in better shape."

Brenna sat on the edge of a cement feed trough, chin planted in her hands, elbows braced on her knees. Freedom stood nearby, his head hanging, his tail swishing at mosquitoes. He didn't usually have to put up with human company at night, but tonight he'd been brushed, combed, rubbed down and had his hooves cleaned and oiled before he'd been brought out under the stars to be used as a sounding board. Brenna couldn't sleep.

"I wonder where Cord went. Of course, it's none of my business, but it's awfully late, and his pickup's still gone." Tilting her head back, she studied the sky, first taking in the stars on the left, then the bright twinklers on the right. This sky was different from the one that hung over the east coast. It had to be. It had twice as many stars in it.

"You know, they used to tell time by the stars. I can't. I have no idea what time it is. But people used to plan their lives by the stars." Wiggling her heel, she made a dent in the soft dirt. Lifting her heel and moving it over a few inches, she made another small hole.

"You've got to understand that Cord's counting on you a lot, and that's why he can't quite relax around you. He feels a little guilty about taking you in, too. You don't hold that against him anymore, do you? He'll take you back up to the mountains, and you can have everything you had and more—the mountains, the mares, good feed, a warm barn. You'll do your best for him, won't you?"

The horse stood still as she approached. She was good to him, and she was welcome to stroke his neck and chase some of the mosquitoes away. Her voice was always quiet, a level softness that made no threats.

"I envy you, Freedom. I'd love to ride in that race. There's nothing quite like pitting yourself against others of your kind and putting everything you've got into proving you're the best. It makes your heart race and your mind soar.

"Of course, we don't want your heart racing. No, sir, you just take it easy on that heart rate." She laughed.

"What am I saying? When have I ever known you to over-exert yourself, hmm? You store energy better than a battery. I'm the one who's been having trouble with my pulse rate lately, and we both know what's causing it, don't we?"

Freedom swung his head around and sniffed Brenna's arm. He snorted, and she laughed again. "I've got nothing to feed you. I wouldn't dare. I don't know what I did to Valiant, but I must have done something. Horses don't founder without a reason. And I was counting on him, just like Cord is counting on you." She thought a minute and added a solemn postscript. "Just like my father is counting on the Sheik. I think Kyle might be right—not that I'm his kid the same as Kyle is, but that the whole thing is silly. I have to sell him Pheasant Run, and at a fair price. I just wanted to show him I could do it. I could take a horse he was going to cull, and I could make a winner out of him." She dropped her forehead against the horse's neck and whispered, "I wanted him to see how good I was."

She stood that way for a long time, mentally changing "him" to "them." She wanted her father's respect. From Cord she wanted that and more. The conversation she'd overheard that afternoon had played itself out again in her head a hundred times, and the silences were louder than the words. "Have you told her you love her?" "What are you afraid of?" No answers.

"Well," she said at last, running a hand over Freedom's jowl, "what time do you suppose it is? You don't care, do you? I guess I do. I guess that's why I'm out here talking to you."

"It's ten after two."

With an inward groan Brenna turned toward the corral fence, knowing exactly what she would see. And there he stood, arm hooked over the corral's top rail, a cowboy hat tilted back from his face and a cocky grin on his mouth.

Damn the man! She never knew when she would turn and find him there listening to every word she said. "How long have you been standing there?"

"Not long." He hoisted himself over the fence and dropped to the ground like a cat. Still grinning, he ambled across the corral in her direction. "Do you think I'd eavesdrop on your conversations with your closest confidant? 'Course not," he said, stopping only inches from her and dropping his face close to hers. "I'm a gentleman."

He smelled of beer and smoke. "I take it you've been socializing," she said tightly.

"Yep. Went out for supper. Had a couple of beers. Danced with a few ladies…"

"I didn't think you smoked."

"I don't. My friends do."

"Are you drunk?"

"Nope."

"Well, you smell like a brewery."

He put his nose in the air and sniffed. "Never been to a brewery. Does it smell much like horse manure? That's all I smell."

"That's because you're standing on the wrong side of my nose." When he laughed she turned away, but Freedom blocked her escape. Cord caught her from behind, and Freedom suddenly decided it was time for him to walk away completely.

Nuzzling the hair at her temple, Cord muttered, "From this side of your nose I smell wildflowers."

Brenna pulled away and followed Freedom, although her steps were slow. "*You* don't smell like wildflowers, believe me."

"Of course not. I'm a man." Stuffing his hands in his front pockets, he shrugged. "Men smell like after-shave and sweat, and sometimes beer and smoke."

What men? she wondered. Not Cord. He usually smelled of Ivory soap, of charcoal smoke from the forge or wood smoke from the fireplace, of leather, of horse sweat, and, yes, his own sweat. But beer and barroom smoke were not his scents. At least, she hadn't known them to be. "Did you have a good time?"

"Yep."

She'd reached the feed trough, which was where she'd left Freedom's lead rope. It was time to put the horse up and go to bed. She really didn't want to know what Cord had been up to until this late hour, she told herself. "I guess you must have closed the joint down."

"Sure did. Haven't done that in a long time."

"I'm sure the *ladies* were glad to have you back in circulation."

"Who said I was ever out of circulation?"

She turned, faced him and squared her shoulders. "You did. You said you hadn't been out in a long time."

"No, I didn't. I said I hadn't closed the joint down in a long time."

His grin was infuriating. "And I said I'm sure the *ladies*, the ones you danced with—the ones who frequent *joints*—were glad to have you back."

"Hoo-wee!" he crowed, taking a step toward her for every one she took backward. "I think *this* lady's jealous."

"Think again—" the backs of her legs met the trough, and suddenly she was sitting in it "—Buster."

"Buster!" Cord hooted. "Is that what the ladies call the men back East? Buster?" Forcing a straight face as he loomed over her, he suggested, "Have a seat, Brenna."

"I did."

"Mind if I join you?"

"Would it matter at all if I did?"

"Nope." He settled in with a satisfied sigh. "This here's

a public trough. This is what you call your rural park bench.''

"I feel silly sitting in a feed trough.''

"Well, you look silly,'' he told her, folding his arms across his chest as he gave her a cursory once-over. "But nobody's looking except me, and I'm sitting in one, too.''

"Yes, but you're drunk.''

"I'm not drunk,'' he assured her. "What's more, I don't get drunk. Did you think I was out raising hell?''

"I didn't give a thought to what you might be doing.'' She scooted forward to sit on the flat edge of the trough, which felt less ridiculous than sitting inside it.

"Then why were you waiting up for me?''

She looked back over her shoulder. His grin was still there. "I was *not* waiting up for you.''

"No? You were out here at two o'clock in the morning talking to a horse, Brenna. What have *you* been drinking?''

"Nothing!''

Chuckling, he joined her on the rim. "Then you were waiting up for me.'' He shook his head, still grinning at her. "Buster? After the crack I made about not being out of circulation, I would've expected *bastard*. Only you would come up with 'buster.'''

"You are so conceited, Cord O'Brien. I've never known a man with such an inflated ego.''

"Then you haven't known many men, honey.'' He sobered and looked down at her, considering. "We've already established that, haven't we? And to be fair, I didn't dance with any *ladies* tonight. I danced a couple of times, but...'' He looked down at the toes of his boots and shook his head. "I lied about having a good time. I didn't.''

"Then why did you stay out so late?'' she asked with a shyness that squeezed his heart.

"I had to give it a fair shot, didn't I?'' He turned her

face toward him with one hand and brushed the hair back from her face with the other. "You look beautiful, you know that?"

Brenna blinked and smiled. "And how many times have you said that tonight, and to how many different *ladies*?"

"Once. And only to one."

She lifted her chin, and he leaned closer. Their lips touched, lightly at first. He tasted of beer, and she tasted of mint toothpaste. These were teasing kisses, holding-off kisses, kisses that said she'd waited, kisses that said he was glad she had. She lifted one hand to his shoulder, and he buried one in her hair and rolled his forehead back and forth against hers, edging his hat a little farther back on his head.

"Anybody ever made love to you in a feed trough?" he whispered.

"Not that I recall. Especially not a *public* feed trough."

"Then I think we'd better find someplace private before I kiss you again. The next one's gonna melt the fillings in your teeth." Sliding his hand down her arm as he stood, he pulled her to her feet and led her across the corral, no longer ambling.

"Where are we going?"

"To the loft."

Hauling back on his hand, she dug her heels into the dirt. "The loft! What's wrong with...with your trailer?"

"It's half a mile away." It wasn't, but he didn't give her the chance to quibble over distance. He was still walking, and he still had her by the hand as he headed for the barn door. With a lurch, she followed.

"What about Freedom?" she asked, looking back.

Cord slid the barn door shut. "'Fraid he can't chaperone tonight. He can't make it up the ladder."

Brenna climbed the ladder, feeling the rush of excitement

she'd known as a child when she found a good hiding place. When she stepped into the loft a cat scurried across her path, bounded over a stack of sacked feed and disappeared. The clerestory window in the big pine-log barn gave them light, and Cord slid the loft door open to give them air. Brenna followed him, her fingertips tingling as she watched him duck under the slanted rafters and break open a square bale. A little work produced a pile of sweet-scented alfalfa. With a quick tug Brenna was in his arms.

"This is crazy!"

"This is fun."

"This is childish."

"In a minute it won't be."

"Cord! What if somebody comes?"

"Who? Daddy?"

"Anybody!"

"Then we'll be very...very...quiet."

"Cord! I don't want to take that off up here."

"I do. Shh."

"Are there any...ummm...mice up here?"

"They're busy playing with the cat."

"What if they...sneak up and bite me on the..."

"They won't. They don't know a good thing when they see it."

"But I feel so..."

"You are. So am I. Oh, God, so am I."

"Oh, Cord...Cord...this is...crazy."

He stood beside the open window, moonlight mixing with the damp sheen on his dusky skin. He was beautiful, and the fact that he stood naked by a barn window—the fact that she lay naked in a pile of hay—now seemed natural. Breathing deeply of the alfalfa and musk scents that drugged her into lethargic contentment, Brenna sighed. She liked this lofty nest. She liked feeling a little daring, a little brash. She liked lying there just looking at Cord.

"Look at that damned horse," Cord muttered, shaking his head.

Brenna's nest rustled as she sat up, hugging her knees. "He doesn't waste any sleeping time. He's probably standing in the corral sound asleep."

"Ordinarily he would be, but he knows I've got you up here, and he's standing down there like a sentry, both ears pricked in this direction." Brenna's soft laughter brought Cord's head around. "You don't think so? If I went down there right now, that horse would punch me in the mouth."

"Only because you wouldn't let me put him back to bed."

"Fact of the matter is I wasn't sure he couldn't make it up the ladder. When you were out there talking to him, I half expected him to answer you." Cord turned from the window and walked back into the shadows, ducking the rafters and treading gingerly with his bare feet. "Ouch!"

"What's wrong?"

Favoring the ball of his left foot, he settled beside her in the nest. "I think I got a splinter."

"The cowboy with tender feet."

"This is serious," he muttered, hiking his foot over the opposite knee and peering down at it in the near darkness.

"This is absolutely crazy," Brenna said, giggling. "But you're right—it's fun."

Putting his foot down, Cord draped his arm over his upraised knee. "You've been around horses long enough. Haven't you ever discovered the magic of lofts?"

"The stables I frequent are owned by other people."

"This one is, too," he reminded her.

"Yes, I…I know it is." The merry lilt had gone out of her voice.

Hugging her legs in front of her, she fixed her chin in the chink between her knees. Her hair fanned over her shoulders, and she looked unaccountably young. She sat there curled up in a ball, shielding her femininity, protecting her vulnerability. Cord wanted to take her in his arms and carry her, just as she was, to some fortified place where he could keep her safe. He watched her lower her forehead to her knees, and he wanted to bite his tongue for having spoken.

"You can be part of it, Brenna. You belong with this family. This is your father, your brother, and Janet is—"

"No," she whispered, rolling her forehead over her knees. Then she lifted her chin, straightened her back and became the woman he had known again. "No. I don't belong with them, not now."

She belonged with *him*, he thought wildly. Why hadn't he said that? *Have you told her you love her? What are you afraid of?* Touch her, at least, he told himself, and he put his hand near her shoulder and stroked her arm. "You're going to ride at Rocky Top," he said, bringing her head around slowly. Her frown asked him what he was talking about. "I want you to ride Freedom."

"You don't owe me anything, Cord." Her eyes met his across the shadows and searched them for guilt.

"This has nothing to do with owing anybody anything."

"What, then?"

"I want Freedom to win that race."

"And you want to ride him to the finish line yourself."

She knew him because she knew herself. They shared that love of competition. He wouldn't try to fool her with any denials. "I wanted to ride Buckshot to the finish line, too, but I didn't make it."

"That wasn't your fault."

"No, but I lost, regardless of whose fault it was. And I reactivated an old problem of mine in the process."

"You said you'd be all right by...you said the pain was gone."

He lifted a shoulder and puckered his mouth, considering the things he'd said. Sure, he would be all right. He always said that. "Valiant's pain is gone, too, but you've got sense enough not to run him."

She studied him for a moment. "Cord, I know how much you want this race."

"That's why I'm asking you to be my jockey. You've trained him, not me. He's your friend. When I ride him, he's like a truck carrying a load of cement blocks. He gets the job done, but he labors up the hill. With you, it's...it's what a woman and a horse do naturally together. At least, *this* woman—" one hand on her arm, he gestured toward the window with the other "—and *that* horse."

Resting her chin thoughtfully against her knees, she kept him under scrutiny. "Your back would give you trouble once you got tired," she reasoned.

"Yeah, it would."

She gave him an indulgent smile. He wanted to ride in that race as badly as she did, and he wasn't planning on getting tired. "Of course, I could come flying out of the saddle on a downhill slide, too."

"You won't. If this course had a suicide slide in it, I wouldn't let you ride."

"Wouldn't *let* me?"

"Wouldn't *ask* you. Wouldn't offer you my horse. Wouldn't sit here on pins and needles—"

"Splinters and hay needles?"

He chuckled, squeezing her arm. She would do it, he thought. "Splinters and *hay* needles, waiting for your answer."

"There are no guarantees," she pointed out. "Something could go wrong for me just as it did for you. I don't want to disappoint you, Cord." And she didn't. God help her, she didn't want to fail him if she took his place in that race.

"You won't." He plucked a small, dry leaf from her hair and touched her cheek. "Freedom will give you the best ride you've ever had."

"That's what he was going to give you," she said. "What will you be doing if you're not riding?"

"I'll be your pit crew," he promised. "Jesse and me. You can't ask for better. Jesse knows how to take care of horses better than most vets."

"And you?"

He slid his hand from her shoulder down her back, letting his fingers play along her spine. "I know how to take care of you." He kissed her shoulder and breathed, "Better than most anybody." Shifting his weight, he turned on his foot and struck the splinter against the floor. He grimaced and sucked his breath through his teeth.

"Let me see if I can—"

"Forget it. It's too damned dark."

"Let me *see*," she insisted, pushing him back to his elbows in the hay. "With my hands, the way you do. I've been watching you feel out those high spots on the horses' hooves. Left foot?"

"Mmm-hmm." Relaxing back on his arms, he decided to suffer her gropings. She was touching him, and that, in itself, was worth a splinter, even if she only touched his foot.

But she had his leg in her hands, and she slid them over the curling hair and the hard calf to his ankle, and then to the ball of his foot. "Here?" Her touch was gentle, skimming lightly over his skin. "Yes, here it is." The splinter was big enough to be managed with the fingernails and in deep enough to require a firm pull. "There."

"Thanks."

"Lie still," she whispered, running her fingertips over the arches of his feet, his ankles, his shins. "Let me make sure that's the only one."

For Cord it was an exercise in mind over matter. He cursed himself silently for his long legs, and her for having only two small hands. How could two small hands perform such delicate brutality? What small strokes, and, Lord! he'd never had knee trouble, but those hands were giving it to him. The cartilage was turning to sponge. Ah, wonderful agony.

When she reached his thighs they went slack, just as he'd made hers do whenever he touched her there. She wanted to feel his muscles tighten under her hands, and she stroked the insides of his thighs until they did. He was magnificent. She continued to stroke his skin with open palms until he groaned. Of course, she knew why. She saw the reason, and she knew she was the cause. But it felt good to touch him, and she wanted to go on touching him just this way. Inch by intimate inch.

Straddling his thighs, she looked up to ask, but she saw the answer in his half-closed eyes. It was all right to touch him there, too. He wanted to be touched as much as she had, and when she did he closed his eyes and showed her the way that was best for him.

Moments later he gripped her wrists and would have pulled her hands from him, but she resisted, whispering a husky, "I've decided...Cord, I've decided..."

"Brenna, let me..."

"No, let me." She moved and sheathed him within herself, then moved again. "I've decided...to be your jockey."

Chapter Ten

Now Brenna and Freedom worked to become a team. They had already become friends, and that was half the battle. A friend wouldn't kick a friend who was hanging on to his tail, and a teammate was willing to tow a fellow teammate uphill using his tail as a tow rope. "Tailing" was just one of the energy-conserving strategies Brenna worked out with Freedom. The horse seemed to take special pleasure in going for a jog when his jockey jogged beside him. When Brenna got winded Freedom would stop to let her climb aboard his back, and then he would lope along for another mile without even breathing hard, just to show her that he could.

"They won't be checking *my* respiratory rate, anyway," Brenna reminded him when she caught her breath. "I can come in gasping and hyperventilating, and we'll have no problem. You're the one who has to pass the vet check."

Brenna knew she and Freedom were everybody's idea of

a longshot. He was inexperienced, and she was a "dude." Being a longshot suited her just fine. If she had Cord's confidence that was all she needed.

Dakota Sheik had over five hundred miles of endurance competition under his cinch, and Henry Sinclair figured he was due for a big win. The handsome Arabian stallion consistently placed high, and Hank didn't race him as often as he might have. During breeding season the stud was kept busy and well fed. Some people believed that a breeding stud was useless for anything besides breeding, but Hank believed in using his horses. His mares were all saddle-broke, and his studs were proven performers. Dakota Sheik was going to be his wonder horse.

Hank wanted to win at Rocky Top. On the other hand, when O'Brien told him that Brenna would be riding the mustang in the race, Hank knew he'd be pulling for her, too—silently, of course. Brenna hadn't forgiven him yet, and he wasn't going to grovel. She would have to make up her own mind about him. Meanwhile he was going to enjoy this race. He had two kids entered, and he knew they were both well mounted.

It was a difficult admission for Hank to make, but that mustang of O'Brien's had turned out to be some horse. He decided—and not without paternal pride—that it was Brenna's doing. His daughter had made a silk purse out of a sow's ear. He'd only intended to give the Sheik a couple of extra days up in the Big Horns before the race started, but watching that tireless mustang work made Hank change his mind. They would go out to the Rocky Top site a week in advance and let the Sheik get his bearings at high altitudes.

Hank, Kyle and Janet had been camped in the Big Horn Mountains for two days before Cord and Brenna arrived. Hank had brought a camper and chosen an improved campsite, while Cord brought a tent, left his pickup and trailer with Hank, and packed the horses for a primitive campsite, one not accessible to motor vehicles. He explained that the training was over and the endurance test was about to begin. To himself he confessed a selfish motive. He wanted Brenna to himself. This was it; this was the culmination of her summer's work. Once the race was over she would be gone. He knew nothing about her world, but he would make damn sure she remembered his.

Many of the campgrounds in the Cloud Peak area were built to accommodate horses. There were split-rail corrals in most and watering facilities in some. Cord had packed some feed, but he knew he would have to make at least one trip back to Hank's campsite for more. He chose a site that had a nice view of the lake and Cloud Peak, but it was isolated and difficult to reach. The ranger had raised an eyebrow at Cord's selection and quipped, "You want the honeymoon suite, huh?"

Brenna didn't complain about the trek. She figured she should hike as much as she rode now. But by the time they'd set up the small nylon tent she felt a little lightheaded. When she stood after tying a corner of the tent to its anchor, she swayed.

"I bet you could use something to eat," Cord offered as he pounded the last of the stakes into the ground with a rock. Brenna shook her head, and he noticed that her face had gone chalky. He went to her quickly and put an arm around her shoulders. "Sit down, honey. It's the altitude."

"I thought I was used to it after being at your place." She hadn't intended to lean on him, but sitting down sounded like a good idea. Through the pines she could see the deep blue water of the lake. It slipped out of view as she lowered herself to the ground with a little help from her friend.

"We overdid it with the hike, and you haven't eaten since lunch, when all you had was a salad." He sat beside her and rubbed her knee to comfort her. "Tonight it's skillet biscuits and canned hash, but tomorrow night—golden trout." The promise was made with a confident smile.

"This won't be a problem, will it? I mean, I'll get used to the altitude again before the race, won't I?"

"A lot of people have trouble with the thin air up here, especially when they start to tire out. If you do, you won't be the only one."

"But you wouldn't have any problem with it."

He shook his head as he rose on one knee. "No, I wouldn't. I'd have that advantage." He rose to his feet and headed for the supply packs. "But I've got some disadvantages tipping the scale against me. Your only problem with the scale will be filling out that hundred and fifty pounds."

"I've worked that out," she told him. "What with the sheepskin I've added to the tack, plus a few little things in a cantle bag, plus my hard hat, my heaviest boots and a little bit extra, we're right on the nose at one fifty."

He'd removed a couple of cans and a couple of plastic bags from the packs, but he turned from them to give her a foreboding look. "A little extra what?"

"Well...weight."

"Where did you put it?"

Sitting cross-legged on the ground, she straightened her back and lifted a noncommittal shoulder. "Where it would do the least harm. On me."

"What are you talking about?"

"I found a way to add a little weight to my boots, that's all." The quizzical expression on his face made her uncomfortable. She was the rider; making the required weight was her problem. "I don't want to add any more dead weight. At least if it's on me, it's live weight."

"How much?"

"Just a couple of pounds," she said off-handedly.

"Put it in the cantle bag."

She didn't like his tone. This wasn't his decision. "I don't want it there. That's over the kidneys. I've worked it all out, Cord, and I have all the extra weight carefully distributed."

"Then you stay in that saddle and let the horse carry it," he ordered, moving closer to her as he became increasingly stern. "If he can carry me, he can damn sure carry a hundred and fifty total. You're not jogging around with weights stuck in your—"

"Cord, I know what I'm doing." Brenna rose to her feet and lifted her chin. "For their size my legs are as strong as yours. I'm not asking Freedom to contend with any more dead weight than necessary."

But she would get tired, he thought as he stood his ground in the stare-down. She would get dizzy. She would push herself too hard, and she wouldn't give up until she keeled over. He had a mental picture of her jogging into a vet check station with ten pound weights strapped to her ankles. Feet dragging in the dust, she would keep her chin up until she handed over the reins, and then she would crumple pathetically to the ground. Though Brenna hadn't actually budged, Cord reached to catch her just as, in his mind, she stumbled into his arms. "Halfway through this race we're going to have a horse without a rider. Be sensible, Brenna."

Shaking his hands off her shoulders, she scowled up at him. "No other rider entered in this race has the training, background and knowledge in this field that I have. 'Sensible' doesn't begin to describe the woman I am, Mr. O'Brien." Her finger punctuated each carefully enunciated word as she tapped it against his chest. "'Sensible' is a wishy-washy word, one that doesn't do me justice. I train with painstaking thoroughness and absolute dedication. I compete with painstaking concentration and absolute passion. Sensible is for beginners. Sensible is for those who are satisfied if they simply manage to finish the race.''

He'd been concerned for her, and her sudden indignation surprised him. Looking down at the accusing forefinger, he shrugged. "To finish is to win in an endurance race, or so they say.''

"I don't know why you asked me to ride your horse in this race, but I don't think it was because you believed I could win for you. And I can.'' She made a fist and thudded it twice against an innocent white button on his blue chambray shirt. "I *can* win for you. It's the one thing…'' It was the one thing she had to give him, the one thing she was sure she had to offer that no one in his right mind would walk away from. She was, after all, one of the most expensive trainers in the business. She looked up and saw doubt in his eyes. "It's what I do well, Cord. Believe me.''

What had he done? Why had his concern for her made her angry with him? Her eyes glittered up at him in the soft light of early evening. Eyes like splintered shards of green glass that could slice open a man's chest and lay his heart bare. He closed his hand around her wrist and stroked her pulse point with his thumb. "I believe you. I've watched you. I just don't want you to think you have to win this race at any cost. That isn't why I asked you to ride.'' He'd wanted to give her this race. Couldn't she see that?

"But that's why I agreed to ride.'' She wanted to give him this race. Didn't he know that?

They stood for a moment, absorbed in each other's eyes. Take this, each one willed. Let me give you what I know you want most.

"You're the rider," he admitted at last. "Do what you think best." *I'll be there when you need me.*

Brenna nodded, letting a hint of a smile enter her eyes. "I think it would be best if I did the dishes tonight. I've never made skillet biscuits."

"Then you need a lesson in camp cooking, Miss Sinclair, and I'm just the man to give it to you," he promised, putting an arm around her shoulders.

"I admit to being a tenderfoot." They were headed for the fire pit, and Brenna put her arm around Cord's waist without giving the action a thought. "I may crow about my strength, but I admit to some weaknesses."

"You don't have to. I think I've got most of them pinpointed." He gave her a little squeeze before he drew away to get the fire started.

"Oh, really?"

"Sure. You like most foods okay, but you're crazy about fish. You get all melty-eyed over wildflowers and wild foxes." He knelt by the grate, arranging pieces of wood from the pile supplied by the park. "I'll bet you don't own a fur coat." She laughed, and he knew he'd guessed right. He scratched a match against the side of a box, and it flared in his hand. "You like fire," he continued, holding the match to the kindling. "You get lost in it, and I can always count on you being soft and mellow when the fire burns low."

Satisfied with his work, he stood and gathered her under his arm again as she watched the young flames leap through the grate. "Out here we'll have a fire every night." It was a husky promise, made close to her ear. "Once you're soft and mellow you have a real weakness for my mustache." It brushed her cheek, and she closed her eyes. "You were curious about it from the first, remember? It was the first part of me you touched, which is why I like to tease you with it before I get down to the more serious business of—''

''Isn't it time for...supper?''

''I didn't bring a watch,'' he murmured before he closed his mouth over hers. She responded immediately, rising to her toes to meet his kiss and return it. If she hungered for anything, it was this. He knew her weaknesses, all right. His tongue's delicate stirring inside her mouth matched the stirring inside her stomach. Reluctantly Cord drew back to suggest, ''Want me to stir something up?'' Brenna blinked once, then managed a small laugh. He grinned, lacing his fingers together behind her back. ''Besides your dander, I mean. I've got a way with biscuits.''

''You've got a way with dander.'' Smiling at the way the innocence in his eyes reminded her of warm, sweet chocolate sauce, she brought her hand from the back of his neck to touch that irresistible mustache.

''Only because I know how to use my mustache. Tickles, doesn't it?''

''Not really.''

He raised one eyebrow. ''What do you mean, not really? Of course it does.''

''How many close encounters have you had with mustaches, Mr. O'Brien?''

''Not many, I guess. There was this one waitress at a truck stop outside Dubois—we used to call her Hulk—anyway, she had a dandy. But you didn't notice it much after you'd been snowed in for three months.'' His eyes twinkled as he exaggerated his drawl. ''Hell, after a bad winter a real pretty woman can be a dangerous shock to a man's system. You wanna break your eyes in easy on somebody like ol' Hulk—somebody with a little hair on her face and hardly any curves.''

Brenna gave Cord's mustache a little tug, and then he said, "Ouch!" and they laughed together.

"What would I be looking for after a winter in the mountains?" she asked saucily. "Someone with hair on his face and hardly any curves?"

"If you were there all winter with me, honey, you'd be looking for summer maternity clothes."

It didn't sound as funny as he'd thought it would. Their eyes locked for a moment, and together they were caught up in a cocoon of possibilities. Given voice, the possibilities became almost tangible. Brenna glanced down at her flat stomach. Cord swallowed audibly. Then she looked quickly past his shoulder, and he glanced past her ear.

There was a husky catch in his voice when he said, "The fire's ready."

They prepared their supper together, taking great care not to step on one another's toes, offering an "excuse me" here, or a "here, let me" there. Glances were quick when they were caught, longer when they seemed to go unnoticed. Something had been uncovered. In jest the cover had been jerked quickly aside, and what they'd seen had startled them both.

He had just been joking, she told herself.

She didn't think much of the idea, he decided.

They ate. The fire burned low. She wasn't mellow, and he saw no point in pressing advantages that weren't there.

They prepared for bed together, again muttering "Excuse me" and being careful not to get in each other's way. Their glances were nervous ones now. The tent was small. Cord had bought an air mattress because he knew Brenna wouldn't sleep well on the ground, and the mattress covered the entire floor.

He'd counted on sleeping close to her. He'd planned on sleeping nude, rather than in his jeans. He'd intended to make love to her every night they spent here. He had accepted the fact that she would be gone soon after the race, and he'd decided that she would be a beautiful memory. But that was before he'd conjured that image of her carrying his child. That was before he'd allowed himself to speak of her as a permanent part of his life, the permanent part that the mother of his child would have to be. Oh, sure, he'd wondered about it, mostly in passing. But he hadn't said it. He hadn't come right out and said it, scared her with it, scared *himself* with it, and ruined everything. Damn him, he'd actually come out and *said* it.

Dressed in a warm sweat suit, Brenna lay still and listened to Cord's breathing. He wasn't asleep; that much she could tell. But she couldn't tell what he was thinking. Did he think she might try to trap him? She should have laughed at what he'd said. He'd meant it to be funny. He'd meant to toss off one of those boasts men used periodically to preen themselves. If she'd laughed along with him, he would have forgotten it, and she would be in his arms right now. Instead she'd imagined herself with his child in her womb. She'd felt it, and she'd looked down to see if it was there. Like a woman in love, she'd felt a deep yearning to bear her man's child. Like a woman in love... Oh, God, she thought, I love him.

The air in the mattress beneath her shifted when he turned to her. Brenna held her breath. His hand stole across the space between them to cover her stomach, and something inside her fluttered.

"I've...*we've* been careful, Brenna."

Her throat burned. "Yes...I know we have."

Brenna moved through the next few days on sheer willpower. This yearning she felt had to be channeled into winning the race. As she explored the mountain trails she concentrated on building a map in her head. With Cord's help, she labeled her map not only with landmarks, but with strategies. Here was a four-mile flat with no shade. Control the speed. Up ahead was a shady path; that was where Freedom could open up. Slow down at the snow fence. Cool off in the creek. Pick up with a slow pace after watering.

This was Brenna's training period, not Freedom's, and it was mental conditioning she sought as well as physical. She noticed that when she got tired, the thin air got to her, just as Cord had said it would. She could expect to have some trouble with that, she decided. It would be a mind-over-matter challenge. Each ride they took was different. They saw a few riders, a few hikers, and lots of wildlife. Each day Brenna became more aware of her surroundings. She cataloged sights and scents and sounds, details she would use, moments she would remember.

Cord was at the center of all those moments. They fished for golden trout, and she remembered the front porch fishing lesson he'd given her, but it didn't help. She would get a nibble, but the fish would be gone by the time she had the presence of mind to take a stab at lodging her hook.

"No wonder I can't catch anything!" she exclaimed, eyeing the tiny hook in disgust. Peering into the tackle box she singled out a larger one. "Let's try this kind."

Cord laughed, shaking his head. "You've got one hell of a mean streak there, lady. How about we finish 'em off with a harpoon?"

"Fine, if it means I eat fish tonight."

"You ate fish last night, didn't you?" She nodded, arms folded over her chest. "And the night before." He put the rod into her hand and motioned for her to cast. She was getting pretty good at that part of it, he noted. "You won't eat any tonight if we use a bigger hook."

Standing behind her, Cord reached over her shoulder and

covered her hand with his own. "These trout only give you one chance. When they hit, you either hook 'em or you lose 'em."

"Hit" seemed a strong word for the quiver that sneaked into their joint grip. Cord flicked the rod quickly, and Brenna ducked out of his way. When he was certain he had supper on the line he brought her into the circle of his arms and let her help reel in their fish.

The wonderful part about cooking fish outdoors was enjoying the aroma, the sizzle, the flavor, and then being done with it. Nothing hung in the air but the scent of pines. Once the skillet and plates had been scoured with sand and the area had been "policed," Brenna and Cord could sit, sip hot campfire coffee and watch the sun slip into the pocket of peaks at the edge of the lake. Brenna was sure the mountain air had special properties, because everything intensified as the sun set—the rich reds and purples in the sky, the robust flavor of the coffee, and the low, velvety timbre of Cord's voice.

"Are you ready for tomorrow?"

She nodded. "One more day of waiting and I think I'd explode. I feel like I've been standing in the starting gate since Christmas."

"Freedom's ready, too." Stretching out on his side, Cord leaned on an elbow. His long legs disappeared into the shadows behind the campfire. "So's the Sheik. I saw him today when I rode down for feed. They moved up closer to the course." Cord grinned at the thought. "Old Hank was bellyaching to beat hell; he had to pitch a tent. He's not much for roughing it."

"The Sheik looks good?" Brenna was surprised at the sound of her own voice. It sounded like a casual question, and she decided the mountain air must have muted her anxiety.

"That horse is no slouch. If I had an interest in breeding and papers and all that, I'd put a mare under him myself." He glanced up, offering an apologetic shrug. He supposed he could have come up with a better euphemism.

"But you are interested in breeding," Brenna reminded him. "You're fussier than anybody. You might as well be raising—what's the name for those little prehistoric horses?"

"Eohippues?" He laughed. "Or is it eohippii?"

"It doesn't matter," Brenna decided, dismissing them with a wave of her hand. "They're long gone."

"But Freedom's not. He's waiting in that corral with a bunch of fancy-blooded horses, probably standing there with his head dragging and his eyes at half-mast."

Brenna giggled. "The other riders probably think he's a hack horse that got in the wrong pen."

"Wait'll they see you. Little bitty wisp of a thing, they'll think—" Cord sat up suddenly, snapped his fingers and reached for his saddle bag. "I brought you something to fatten you up."

"Fatten me up?" A bag of marshmallows landed in her lap. "I promised Freedom I wouldn't—" a package of chocolate bars followed "—make a pig of myself—" last came a box of graham crackers, followed by Cord's broad smile "—at his expense. S'mores?"

"What else?"

Smiling, Brenna gathered the ingredients, and Cord produced two green willow sticks. "The only thing I really liked about summer camp besides the horses were s'mores."

"Ol' Jesse and me did a lot of camping, and he's got a real weakness for sweets." As he loaded marshmallows on the sticks he watched Brenna break crackers and chocolate bars apart. She laid the pieces together on the paper bag he'd brought them in, and then she sat back on her heels, admiring her work and licking her fingers one by one, like a little girl. He smiled. "But then, so do I."

They were both like children as they made and ate their treat. They admired the marshmallows they managed to brown to perfection, teased each other over those they torched, fed one another, and smacked their lips with delight. The first s'mores were gobbled with relish, but the last ones went slowly and were put into perspective alongside s'mores of the past. These were the best ever, they decided.

"It's late, honey," Cord said at last. "You need your rest."

He rubbed his hand over the back of her neck as they sat side by side, watching the last of the coals. Brenna knew there was something else she needed more. They'd slept just as they sat—side by side and fully dressed—every night since they'd been here. The mountain air had been soothing, tranquilizing, and she always slept well once she closed her eyes and gave up the wait. During the night they found one another and held each other as they slept. But Brenna knew she wanted more, maybe more than Cord was willing to give.

"I'm ready." A sigh betrayed her restiveness.

"Jitters?" His fingers kneaded her muscles gently.

"No. Just...anxious for the preliminaries to be over and the main event to be under way."

He nodded, adding a quick laugh. "I know what you mean. You make a hell of a team, you and Freedom."

"I think we have a good chance of winning."

He lifted a shoulder, but he reassured her with a one-handed squeeze. "You have a great chance of doing very well. Take everything as it comes and enjoy the challenge. Don't miss anything. Feel the speed and the wind and the trail, and enjoy pushing yourself just a little farther than you ever thought you could go. It'll be a great ride for you, Brenna." He smiled, and she saw then just how much he wanted for himself this chance he'd given her. "Freedom will give you the best ride you've ever had."

"Second best," she said quietly, and when he frowned, she added, "You were the best I've ever had." She slipped her arms around him and laid her cheek against the breast pocket of his denim jacket.

He hesitated only a moment before he put his arms around her, too. "Is that what you need tonight?" He felt her nod against him. God, he'd been through hell these past few nights! "Do you want preliminaries, or just the main event?"

"I want you."

He lifted her face in his hands and read her need in her eyes. He'd awakened that need in her, he thought. He'd roused a sleeping passion, and now it stared him in the face, hungry, expecting satisfaction. *In another few days she'll be walking out on you, O'Brien.* He swept his thumb over her lower lip and felt her tentative smile. What the hell, he thought. Tonight she wanted him. She smelled of wood smoke and pine pitch, and her skin was soft and warm beneath his hands, and there was no damned way he could deny her anything. Lowering his head, he loved her lips with the touch of his.

He drew her to her feet and undressed her there, in front of the tent. Buttons came away from their holes one by one, and only the backs of his fingers touched her. The snap on her jeans was released and zipper teeth separated bit by bit, but only his thumbs brushed her hips as he slid her jeans over them. That light touch coaxed her stomach into a tight coil, but she could say nothing. He'd begun weaving that crystal spell, and she wanted nothing to break it.

Standing nearly naked in the moonlight, Brenna felt wonderfully bold and beautiful. He honored her vulnerability with gentleness. His gaze foreshadowed hot demands, but there was reassurance in the care he took with her. He unveiled her breasts and watched the nipples pucker as the chilled air touched them. She could hardly breathe. He could hardly think.

The single word in his mind was an impossibility, and he hid his face between her breasts, hoping to drive the word away. Her nipples tightened as he tasted them with his tongue, but the word was still there. He slipped to his knees, buried his face in her belly. He would let passion push the word away and he used his hands and his mouth to build it in her while its flames leaped and licked inside him.

She was trembling when he took her to the tent. They struggled together with his clothes. Her impatient groan became one of pure pleasure when his skin slid against hers. He felt so good, and all she could do was feel. She felt him find her, felt him fill her, and felt the glory of the pleasure he took within her.

And when he was spent and lay with his head on her breast, Cord still had the word in his head. He had the taste of it in his mouth, the smell of it in his nose, and the feel of it on his skin. He heard it in her heartbeat. The passion cooled, but the warmth was still there. He loved her.

The rising sun caught them sleeping. Cord awoke gradually, comfortable inside the brightening yellow shell of the tent. Brenna still slept in his arms. He turned his face into a soft tumble of strawberry blonde hair and smiled. She had a habit of waking before he did, but on this day of all days she slept. He didn't want to awaken her. He wanted to lie there, holding her while she slept, enjoying the feeling that she was his. Within this small shell she *was* his. Here they fit together perfectly. Wasn't there a rhyme about a guy who put his wife in a pumpkin shell? "And there he kept her very well." Cord could see how that might work.

He brushed her hair back from her face, and she stirred against him. Tilting her head back, she found his face with sleepy eyes and smiled.

He kissed her. "Sleep well?" His greeting was morning husky.

"Umm-hmm. Somebody must've given me a sleeping potion last night." She stretched, and the hair on his legs tickled her. "My own special brand."

"Is it habit-forming?"

"You tell me."

Like a cat stretching after her nap she rose above him on her arms, her hair draped over one side of her neck. Her green eyes were soft with contentment, and she purred. "Too early to tell." Pulling her knees under her, she sat up and smiled down at him. "The drug needs further testing. If I become addicted it probably isn't safe for mass consumption."

Reaching to take her bare shoulders in his hands, he thought she would make a lovely sculpture—a woodland nymph perched on a mushroom. "It isn't available for mass consumption," he said, distracted by the beauty of her breasts.

He was pulling her down, and she was resisting only to contribute to the game. "Is this one of those limited offers?" she asked, smiling.

Her breast met his mouth. "Ummm."

"How much more time, ah, is there?"

"I didn't wear a watch," he reminded her. She braced her hands on his shoulders as he lifted her on top of him.

Part of the game was to return as many sensible answers as possible while he nuzzled her breasts. "How do you keep time?"

"I can't keep it." He was through playing. "So I take it."

It was hard to predict how long a hundred-mile race would take, since so many conditions affected the outcome. Riders could expect to average about thirteen miles per hour over flat terrain, but they would do well to achieve six in the mountains. The time they spent at the checkpoints would make the difference individually, and weather conditions affected everybody. Cord and Brenna emerged from their yellow cocoon into a melting haze and bright yellow sunlight. Brenna breathed deeply. The air tasted fresh, and her skin tingled with the crispness of it. She would take the day just as it was and make it hers.

"I can't eat," she warned, watching Cord whip a fork through a batch of eggs in the skillet.

"You *think* you can't. Starting right now, you let me decide what you can and can't do while you're on the ground. You don't even have to think about it."

"I never eat when I'm competing." The smell of the food didn't even appeal to her. She sat on the ground to pull her boots on. She wore riding breeches, a long-sleeved cotton shirt to protect her arms from sun and scratches, and a hard hunt cap.

Cord transferred the food to their plates. She would eat fish and eggs, high in protein and cooked with absolutely no fat. He would see that she got carbohydrates and electrolytes when she needed them, and he would measure each bite and count the number of times she chewed. He handed her a plate. "*We're* competing this time, Brenna. You, me and Freedom. You've never worked with a coach before, have you?"

The corners of Brenna's mouth turned down as she eyed the eggs. "No."

"You have to trust me. Have total faith in my judgment. No arguments. No grandstanding. Got it?"

"I'm the rider."

"You're the rider," he agreed. "And I'm the coach."

Reluctantly she took up the fork. "You're the coach."

Thirty-eight horses and riders gathered in a grassy meadow, and there was anxiety in the air. Hot-blooded horses, made more nervous by anxious riders, wasted energy with their prancing and pawing. Seasoned horses waited more patiently while riders and their gear were weighed and a preliminary vet check was done on each horse. Prerace conditions were established for each horse, and those conditions would be compared with the animal's metabolic signs at each of the six vet checkpoints during the race. The course had to be completed within twenty-four hours.

"Where've you two been? Been lookin' for you since before sunup." Jesse had been pacing like one of the hot-blooded breeds. He'd agreed to help out, but he didn't like the idea of putting Brenna up in this race, not one bit. He thought he'd raised Cord better. A man didn't put his woman to work when he couldn't get the job done himself. But here was Cord, smiling like he'd just won the Irish Sweepstakes, and that little bit of a girl didn't look scared at all.

"Freedom wasn't anxious to stand around shooting the breeze with the rest of the studs," Cord said.

"I hope the ornery cuss takes a bite out of the vet and

gets himself disqualified. Brenna, you got no idea what you're in for, honey.'' Jesse turned a pointed glare on Cord. "But you do, mister, and there ain't no excuse. No excuse for you, and that's my final word.''

"You don't know what 'final' means, Jesse.'' Cord laid a hand on the old man's shoulder. "We're counting on you.''

Jesse touched the brim of his battered cowboy hat in deference to Brenna. "You can count on me, ma'am. Used to be a lady could always count on a cowboy to be a gentleman. I thought I'd raised him better.''

Cord raised his brow at the thumb that was jerked his way. "You brought everything in the four-wheel drive?'' Disgusted, Jesse nodded. "Then forget about ladies and gentlemen. She's the rider, and we're her pit crew. And we're about to live one hell of a long day.''

Freedom didn't like the vet, and Jesse's wish very nearly came true. The doctor narrowly escaped the mustang's long incisors. Brenna breathed a sigh of relief when she led the horse away from the examination station, her starting number in hand. She was among the last to mount up and take her place. She kept Freedom well away from the other horses, preferring to stay back from the starting line. Some horses would explode at the start, but Freedom wouldn't. The quickstarters would soon be left behind.

A familiar grin among the riders caught Brenna's attention. Kyle was wide-eyed with excitement, and Brenna smiled back, because she knew the feeling. He gave her a wink and a thumbs-up gesture, and she heard herself call out, "Good luck, Kyle!'' He nodded, jerking his chin toward the sidelines as Dakota Sheik shifted beneath his rider. Brenna turned to catch a wave from Janet and a nod from Henry Sinclair. The smile she returned came easily.

And then Brenna found Cord's face in the crowd of spectators. He'd asked her to have faith in him. There she sat in his horse's saddle, entered in the race he wanted more than anything to win. He'd put his faith in her. He gave her a thumbs-up sign, and she smiled. And then the starting gun was fired.

Chapter Eleven

Brenna's heart skittered at the signal as Freedom plunged into action. The pack surged across the open flat, and Brenna turned her face to welcome the impact of the wind. She'd put herself abreast of the rest, not aiming for the front but hoping to stay clear. In the excitement Freedom wanted to charge, and Brenna had a wild notion to give him his head, to burst ahead with the wind in her face and her hair flying free. But she controlled the notion, just as she controlled her mount. Her hair stayed tucked under her hat, and she set her mind on pacing herself for the hundred miles ahead.

The course was designed for a fast start, but the sandstone hills soon set the competitors back on their heels for less speed. The Arabians loved this terrain, and Brenna reminded herself that she was pitting her mustang against the course, not against the other horses. As the pack stretched out it was easier to forget about the rest. The wind filled her ears with its rushing roar, staccato hoofbeats adding their pounding rhythm. Brenna looked down as Freedom bore to the right where the trail curved around a sandstone tower. Rock and brush streaked under his feet in a gray blur. Brenna felt the quick rush of power she always borrowed from her horse's speed.

Freedom wasn't interested in drinking the first water they came to. Brenna had taught him to stand in it while she sponged his head and neck, and he'd learned to welcome the attention, though he'd hardly worked up a sweat. She noticed that no one skipped the stream entirely, and some horses drank. Since Freedom hadn't, Brenna resumed at a quicker pace.

At the first checkpoint Freedom's metabolic recovery was accomplished in less than two minutes, but a fifteen minute hold was mandatory. Jesse moved quickly to shoot electrolytes into Freedom's mouth with a syringe, while Cord checked his hooves and legs, and Brenna loosened the girth and lifted the saddle to cool the horse's back.

Cord handed Brenna a small can of apple juice with a soft-spoken order. "Drink slowly."

She complied. "He stops sometimes." Watching Jesse rearrange the thick sheepskin pads that cushioned the saddle on Freedom's back, she reported the phenomenon between sips of juice. "It's funny. He stops for just a couple of seconds, and then he's off at a dead run again."

"You see them do that when you're chasing a herd on a wild horse roundup," Cord told her. "It must be a survival instinct. Are you trying to push him through it?"

Brenna shook her head, draining the can. The cool drink bathed her tongue with its tart sweetness. "He only did it a couple of times after we'd been moving hard. I figured he knew what he was doing."

"He was hardly winded. How about you?"

The excitement in his eyes matched hers. He took pleasure in her passion, just as he did in their lovemaking. Impulsively Brenna laid her hand along his cheek, and he bent his head for her quick kiss. "I'm having a wonderful time."

In a flash she was off again.

There were six vet checks during the race, and the leaders were separated only by minutes after the first two. The steep ascents and descents became harder to negotiate as the race wore on, but these mountains were Freedom's country. The other horses found relief in the occasional alpine meadows, but they bored the plucky mustang. He slipped through narrow forest trails like a snake and challenged the rocky inclines with the sure-footed ease of a mountain goat.

Freedom drank water at every opportunity now. At the third vet check Brenna ate a sandwich and an oatmeal cookie, and drank as much Gatorade as she could manage. Her admiration for her mount increased as she felt her own stamina stretch.

"He changes leads without any argument," Brenna told Cord as she watched him massage her calves and feet. Freedom favored the left lead, which was something like being left-handed, but Brenna signaled him to lead with his right foreleg periodically to even the strain. "And he exhales in perfect rhythm with his trot."

Cord rolled Brenna over on the blanket he'd spread on the grass. He grinned at her behind her back. She, too, offered no argument as he massaged her thighs and buttocks. "You mean after all this training you're surprised?"

"After all this training I'm still amazed at the way he works."

"So am I," he admitted. "He wouldn't do a damn thing for me."

Jesse called for her, and Brenna squirmed out of Cord's hands. Jamming her hat back on her head, she smiled down at him. "He loves me, Cord. There's no other explanation."

Freedom stood quietly while Jesse gave Brenna a leg up into the saddle. "I don't blame him," Cord muttered to himself as he watched. "I'd run a hundred miles for you, too."

The checkpoints were about sixteen miles apart, but now the miles were passing more slowly. Brenna saw only the same eight or ten horses on the trail now, and one of those was the Sheik. She and Kyle waved at each other as they sponged their horses in a stream. Courtesy and good sense dictated keeping them well apart to prevent distractions. The Sheik seemed to be faring well.

Brenna always dismounted and led Freedom to water and resumed the ride at a slow pace. She kept tabs on his pulse by checking the large artery behind his knee, or by putting her palm over his heart. As the altitude increased it was her own fatigue that took its toll. When she tailed Freedom up an incline she knew his strength carried them both.

About a quarter of a mile from the fourth vet check Brenna slid to the ground and began her trot. Freedom's recovery would begin as soon as she did this, and she wanted a quick check. This was where she gained time, because the other horses were much slower to recover now. She told herself to ignore her own dizziness, that it would go away, but her head swam, and inky confusion clouded her vision. Staggering to the edge of the trail, she fell to her knees and saw the world go black.

When she lifted her head she saw a purple aster peeking up at her through the grass. She took a slow, deep breath, exhaled just as slowly, and felt her head clear. Her field of vision increased to include the tree behind the aster. She sat back on her heels, hoping no one would come by for at least another minute, and she squeezed her hand around the reins.

"If we lose it'll be my fault, Freedom. You're doing fine." The horse nudged her shoulder with his muzzle, and she smiled. "You go on ahead. I'll meet you at the checkpoint." He took two steps back, drawing the reins taut between them. "All right," she sighed, "but you'll have to carry me in this time." Freedom waited while Brenna dragged herself to her feet, and then he shifted to a low spot beside the trail, leaving her standing on the high ground. Despite her shakiness Brenna laughed. "I could swear there's a human being inside you sometimes." With the added height she was able to pull herself into the saddle.

Someone was always assigned to watch the trail and announce the numbers of the incoming riders, alerting the pit crews to be ready. Cord had already decided this would be a longer respite, no matter how incredible Freedom's recovery rate, but when he saw that Brenna was still in the saddle his resolve redoubled. He made a move to help her dismount, but her look told him that she would do it under her own steam. She loosened the girth herself, then let Jesse take Freedom to the vet, who stood waiting, stethoscope in hand.

Cord led Brenna to the spot where the four-wheel drive Jeep Jesse had brought was parked. "I don't feel like sitting, and I don't feel like eating," she warned.

He knew the altitude had gotten to her. She was chalk white, and he could feel that telltale trembling when he put his arm around her shoulders. She wasn't up to this, and he was the one who'd gotten her into it. "Lie down," he ordered in a voice that had gone tight in his throat.

"As soon as we know what Freedom's numbers are I want to see that he—"

"Jesse knows what he needs." Cord's face was grim, and Brenna succumbed to the pressure of his hands on her shoulders, allowing herself to lie down on the blanket because he would have it no other way. "You're not doing another sixteen miles on an empty stomach. We'll take it easy and start with a soft drink.''

He was disgusted with her, she thought. He'd counted on her to be the rider she'd claimed to be, and she'd let a little thin air get to her. If Cord's horse lost this race there would be nobody to blame but herself. Obediently she took the drink, the salt tablet, the fruit, and finally half the sandwich he provided. Then she lay quietly beneath his hands while he massaged every aching muscle in her body.

''You remember when you did this for me?'' he asked, gently kneading the knots in her lower back.

Brenna closed her eyes. The blanket felt rough against her cheek, but his hands felt like a warm balm, and she thought she wouldn't move from that spot ever again. ''I remember.''

''This is how good it felt.''

''Mmmm.''

''You can't appreciate it until you really need it.''

''I really need it,'' she groaned. He'd found the saddle-worn muscles in her buttocks again.

''I know.'' I can give you a lot of things you really need, he told himself, and then he shook the thought from his head. ''How much running did you do this leg?''

''I had to do some tailing…mmm…a little jogging.''

''Let him carry you, Brenna. You're hardly even taxing him. Let him do the work.''

''He's doing the work, Cord. Doing it beautifully.'' She turned her head to the other side, just to keep everything balanced. ''We're going to win this race. I can feel it.''

''Are you still having a wonderful time?''

Half of her smile was lost in the blanket. ''It just gets better and better.''

''Then how about another sandwich?''

What had begun with ready energy had become a trial in the truest sense. Brenna had been prepared to try the horse against the course, but now she tested herself. She measured herself against the map of the course and mentally parceled out a piece of energy to cover each mile that remained. What had begun as a crisp morning had gone from a humid afternoon to a drizzly evening.

Brenna plunged ahead, telling herself that she was glad the hot, clammy air was well behind. But the air grew chilly and she was soaked through to the skin. The sheepskin that padded the saddle became soggy, and Brenna was soon sitting on a sponge.

None of this bothered Freedom. Every sixteen miles or so Jesse turned up with his bran mash. Freedom had learned that he could count on Brenna to know where to find Jesse; all Freedom had to do was get there. Mud was only a minor inconvenience along the way.

"That horse doesn't quit, does he?" Kyle kept the Sheik a respectable distance away in order to keep both horses calm, but he trotted within shouting distance of Brenna, having passed her and been passed by her several times during the race.

"Neither does that one," Brenna acknowledged.

"The Sheik doesn't like the steep stuff, but he eats up the flats." Kyle grinned. "You look wet."

"I feel wet," Brenna tossed back lightly. "How about you?"

"I'm never going out in the rain again—not even to get the mail!" Kyle's saddle had sheepskin padding, too, and Brenna noted that the Ace bandages he'd wrapped around his knees, both for protection and to keep his jeans from creeping up, were now black with mud. His cowboy hat offered him some shelter from the rain. "Dad says Freedom's recovery rates are setting records. He's telling anyone who wants to listen how you made a silk purse out of a sow's ear."

"Freedom was never a sow's ear."

"He was never an Arab, either, which is the only breed Dad believes in. He's pretty impressed."

Brenna decided to save that information for consideration at a later time—a time when she wasn't too tired to be defensive. There was only one thought that she wanted to keep in her brain right now. "If we keep this up, one of us is going to win this thing, Kyle."

"If we keep this up, neither one of us can lose." Kyle looked as though he believed in what he said. "I'm pulling ahead now. This is the Sheik's best terrain. Hang in there, Brenna."

Brenna watched her brother pick up an easy gallop and pull away across the meadow. Her brother, she thought. She wanted him to fare well. If we keep this up…hang in there…if we keep this up, neither one of us can lose.

Kyle had looked as tireless as Freedom. The Sheik was pushing it, but Kyle was still out for a Sunday ride. Brenna had trained herself to endure distance, but not rain. She was cold and wet, and "hanging in there" was a perfect description of what she was doing—like something limp dangling from a clothesline.

The evening had turned from smoke gray to slate when Brenna slid from the saddle into Cord's arms. He swept her into his embrace and carried her to the Jeep, and it felt so good she didn't protest. The Jeep was parked in a copse of trees, the motor running and the heater warming its interior. Cord put Brenna in the back, climbed in after her and began undressing her immediately. Brenna turned herself over to him—in the interest of efficiency, she told herself. At this point it would have been difficult for her to decide which leg to remove from her pants first.

"I think this rain gives Freedom an advantage." Brenna watched her wet clothes being peeled away as though she were a third-party observer. Her mind replayed the last leg of the course. ''That last descent through the rocks is going to be slippery, isn't it?''

''Probably,'' Cord answered without looking up from his job. He had her riding breeches down to her knees when he felt her whole body shiver. He hurried to get them off.

''Do you have a towel handy? I'm cold.''

''I know. I'm going to take care of that.'' He wrapped her hair in one towel and rubbed another one over her quickly. Then he draped a blanket over her shoulders and began a thorough, all-over massage.

Brenna moaned appreciatively. ''This makes it worth it.''

''Oh, yeah? How about if I drive this jalopy over the hill and really make it worth it?''

She closed her eyes and let a smile drift in. ''Soon as we collect our awards. How're we doing on time?''

''Excellent. I'm satisfied that we've each made a point.''

Pushing herself to her elbows, Brenna looked down at the hands that were rubbing warmth in her thighs. ''So?''

The hands stilled as Cord lifted his dark head. His eyes glittered in the darkness. ''So you've had enough.''

''Enough what?'' Her tone was incredulous.

''Enough rare air, enough rain, enough race.'' He kneaded her thighs slowly, hypnotically, and he spoke quietly. ''Your coach is taking you out of the game.''

''Everyone is tired, Cord. It's been a long day. I'm not the only one.''

''You're the only one who's riding for me, and I'm calling a halt.''

''No, you're not.'' Sitting up, she grabbed his wrists and stared at him intently. ''You can't. I won't stop. *You can't stop me.*''

He gave her half a smile. ''You don't think so?''

Her eyes widened. She was going to *win* this race. Didn't he know that? ''Why? You asked me to do this. Why?''

Leaning toward her, he shook his head and took her face

in both hands. It felt tiny, her neck slight, her skin too cool to the touch. "I wasn't counting on rain. I wasn't counting on seeing you come in looking so...tired." *Fragile* was the word that had actually come to mind, but he knew better than to say it.

"That's part of it, Cord. You get tired, and you keep going. Pretty soon you're exhausted, but you keep going. You push yourself a little farther than you ever thought you could go. You promised me that chance, remember?"

He sighed. He knew he had no right to stop her if she insisted on going ahead. "Then take it easy," he said finally. "Winning isn't that important."

"Then what is?" she shot back. "Why did you ask me to ride for you? Didn't you think I had a better chance of riding Freedom to a first-place finish than you did?"

With a shrug he slid his hands to her shoulders and resumed his methodical massaging. "I thought it was important to you to ride in this race. I wanted you to have that opportunity."

"And what about your opportunity?" she asked quietly.

"There's always another one down the road."

Brenna chose not to think about the number of ways she might interpret that comment. Instead she informed him, "This one is mine. You can tell me when to eat, when to drink, when to pick up the pace or slow it down, but you can't tell me when to quit."

He dismissed the urge to attempt a stare down. The spunk in her eyes was indomitable. "Okay, kid. You take the ball and trot with it. But you're going to eat now, and have something to drink. And then I'm going to put my poncho on you, and you're going to sit in that saddle and let the horse who loves you carry you all the way. No more jogging for you."

"Yes, coach," Brenna agreed with a demure smile. She

hadn't done very much jogging lately anyway. "I have one question."

"What's that?"

She opened the blanket just enough to give him a shadowy glimpse of her breasts. "Do I get to wear something underneath the poncho, or am I doing Lady Godiva in the rain?"

Cord watched the trail until his bright yellow rubberized poncho disappeared from sight. Brenna's back was as straight as ever, but he knew how tired she was. She was beyond fatigue. Her muscles were burning energy she didn't have, energy she was mentally borrowing against a future allotment.

"That little girl's pushing the limit," said a voice at Cord's shoulder. He half thought it might be the voice of his own conscience, but it was Jesse. Cord nodded, still watching the trail. "Wonder what she's doin' it for," Jesse added with a thoughtful frown.

The Sheik was slower to recover this time, and Hank walked him while Kyle stood ready to remount the minute his horse was ready. Cord strode through the thickening mud to confront Hank. As he matched his stride with the other man's, he knew he was breaking a cardinal rule of racing etiquette by interrupting Hank's efforts, but the whole idea of racing a horse through a hundred miles of these mountains suddenly struck him as insane, along with any cardinal rules that might go with it.

"She's exhausted, Hank, and she's chilled to the bone." Hank looked up at Cord, but offered no comment. "The altitude got to her early on, and I think that weakened her. I asked her to give it up, but she wouldn't listen."

Hank continued to stare at Cord, his expression unreadable. "What do you want me to say, O'Brien?"

"Say?" Cord barked. "Well, for God's sake, you're her father, Hank."

"And who are you?"

"I'm her...her friend. I don't want to see her get hurt."

"She's been riding most of her life." Hank slid a hand under the Sheik's chest. "Can you see your watch, O'Brien? Give me a thirty-second count, will you?"

Cord looked down at his own bare wrist and then muttered an oath under his breath. "I'm not wearing a watch. Look at that trail, man. Look at the sky."

"Well, she's gone now," Hank said matter-of-factly, then lifted his voice beyond Cord's shoulder. "Kyle, give me a thirty-second count."

"I couldn't just take Freedom away from her, Hank. I couldn't do that. But, damn, I should have stopped her somehow. She just wouldn't listen to me."

Hank was counting heartbeats. "I think he'll pass now, Kyle." Hank watched his son lead his prize horse toward the veterinarian. They were doing well, he thought. They might not win, but they were going to be in the running. He turned his attention back to Cord, who was peering into the darkening sky, water dripping steadily from the brim of his hat. "She just wouldn't listen to you, huh?" Hank offered. "Maybe you weren't saying what she wanted to hear."

"I told her I didn't care about winning!"

Hank smiled, and Cord wanted to hit him. "Did you tell her what you *do* care about?" The lack of an answer settled the question. "That girl's dealing with two cowards, O'Brien. You and me. She's riding her heart out to try to prove something to us—something both of us were too thick-headed to accept on its own merit. Now we've got to let her finish this her way. We've got no right to interfere."

"I've got a right," Cord grumbled. "I got her into this."

"Don't you have any faith in her?" The question

brought a scowl. "I guess that's one of the things *we* have to prove to *her*. You love her every bit as much as I do, O'Brien, and neither one of us has had the nerve to let her in on the secret."

The scowl blackened. Hank had his nerve, all right. Cord wasn't about to share in Hank's well-deserved feelings of guilt. "If you've got some amends to make to your daughter, you'd better stand on your own two feet and make them, Hank. She's leaving after this is over, going back to all that property she inherited from her mother. Any secrets I might have—" Cord noticed Kyle reaching for his saddle horn. "Hey, Kyle!" Shouldering past Hank, Cord barked an order. "You watch out for your sister. If she gets into trouble out there you stop and help her, and the race be damned."

Kyle gave Cord one of his ingenuous grins. "I doubt if I'll even catch up to her now."

Freedom carried her. If anyone ever asked her, she would say that Freedom carried her through the darkness and into the light. Brenna planned the words she would write about this experience. She would describe the bone-melting fatigue, the aches, the soreness, but she would also show the exhilaration. She had become one with Freedom, and they had conquered mile after mile.

Freedom discounted the mire and kept the trail under his feet. As the sky lightened Brenna heard a horse approaching from behind, and she turned to watch a riderless Sheik trot past. A few yards ahead of her, he stepped on his own rein and stopped himself. Brenna caught him easily, her mind racing. Kyle was back there somewhere, maybe walking, maybe not. He might be hurt. There was no decision to be made. Backtracking, she led the Sheik along the muddy trail until she came upon her brother. He was covered with mud, but his own brisk trot made it obvious that he wasn't hurt.

"We slipped in the mud," Kyle explained, taking his horse's reins. "Fell flat on my face. You shouldn't be backtracking now, Brenna. You've almost got this thing in the bag." He shooed her on her way. "Get going!"

"I thought you might be hurt," she explained as she wheeled Freedom back on track.

"I'm okay. Get a move on!"

Brenna moved, all right. She felt a new surge of energy pulse through her veins. The last of the trail was a tricky descent through a maze of angular boulders. No other horse could negotiate it with Freedom's finesse. Long before she reached the finish, Brenna knew she would be first. She lifted her chin and caught the cheers and the wind in her face with a broad smile before she attended to her last test—to trot Freedom out for the vet to prove that he'd run a sound race.

Freedom wouldn't budge. The race was over, and he knew it. He lowered his neck, let his ears sag to half-mast, planted all four feet and stood there. But Brenna had a reserve of patience, and after a few words to assure him that he really only had to take a few more steps, she had him trotting again.

"That was a fine race, Brenna. I never saw one run any better." Henry Sinclair offered a handshake first, but it became a bear hug, which Brenna accepted easily. She had won, and she had it coming. Jesse offered much the same. Janet's arms were open to her, too, with no apparent thought for the fact that it was Brenna and not her son who had ridden in first. Moments later Kyle appeared, and another hug was in the offing. But it was Cord Brenna searched, and she found him at the edge of the crowd. She went to him, reached for him, and her feet were soon dangling above the ground as she was caught in his arms.

"I should have known you could do it," he whispered.

She leaned back until she could see his face, her eyes shining. "You should have known *we* could do it. You, me, Freedom and Jesse. But mostly Freedom," she added quickly.

"Mostly you and Freedom."

The hammer clanked rhythmically against the anvil, filling Cord's ears with the noise of his livelihood. After all the awards had been handed out and the winners' praises sung, he'd brought Brenna back to Pheasant Run, where she had literally collapsed. He hadn't seen her in two days, and he'd been told that for most of that time she'd slept. And during all of that time he'd waited.

Another sound filtered through the harsh clanging, and the hammer stilled in his hands. Piano music, the melody of *Für Elise*, drifted across the paddocks. Cord laid his hammer down and went to the trailer to clean up. He smiled to himself, remembering Hank's advice. "Comes a time when a man's gotta listen to the music."

She played several songs while he washed and changed his clothes, but always she came back to "Für Elise," as though it were a theme gently threading its way through the afternoon breeze. Cord followed the sound to the living room, and smiled when she turned toward the doorway at the sound of his footsteps.

"I came to listen," he said simply.

She returned to the keyboard and played the song once more from the beginning, while he sat on the couch and studied her. She wore royal blue, which brightened her face and accented the strawberry blond hair that curled about her shoulders. She'd been pale when he'd last seen her, but now her own soft peach coloring was back in her face.

Brenna played because she knew that when she stopped they would have to talk. She remembered Jesse's comment

that Cord didn't ask anything a woman couldn't give, and
he'd never asked a woman to stay. The moment when he
would either ask or he wouldn't was at hand. She'd put it
off as long as she could, but now the music had ended and
the talk would begin.

She came to sit next to him.

His lips curved only slightly with the smile of approval
that sparkled in his dark eyes. "You're looking much better
than you were the last time I saw you. I take it Janet feeds
you better than I do."

"You're both persistent," she said, feeling the nervous
strain in the smile she returned.

"Well, you were beginning to look like one of those kids
they paint on velvet—all eyes and no flesh."

"Especially after the altitude started getting to me."

"Especially then. That was when I started kicking myself."

"Why? I was up to it. Nobody comes out of something
like that without a little wear. Have you seen Kyle?"

Broadening his grin, Cord nodded. "He can't handle a
chair yet. Takes his meals at the kitchen counter."

"The Rocky Top trial was one of the most demanding
experiences of my life, and one of the most rewarding."
The comment sounded like the beginning of one of her
articles, and she searched for more personal words. "I want
to thank you for that, Cord."

Cord glanced down at the hands she'd clasped tightly in
her lap. "You showed everybody what Freedom and his
breed can do."

"I'm going to write about it, too. My journal tells an
exciting story about...the horse who loves me." She gave
a nervous little laugh.

"So you won your bet."

Brenna laughed again, tossing her hair with a quick
shake of her head. It was the first sign Cord had seen that

she might, at some point during this reunion, relax a bit. "That was silly. Pheasant Run belongs to my father. He built it. I think maybe we can be friends now, but this is his home." She cocked her head and offered a bright little smile. "And my home is fifteen hundred miles from here. It's time I was getting back. I was going to leave tomorrow morning. Morning flights are so much better than waiting until the day is shot. I couldn't get decent connections, and I don't want to put up with those long layovers. I won't get home until—"

"Home?"

She glanced at him quickly. "Yes, home. Connecticut."

"What have you got there, Brenna?"

"Well...I've got...my life."

Cord shook his head slowly. "Your life is here. Your family is here."

Brenna smiled, remembering the way Janet had fussed over her during the last two days. She'd felt so secure in Janet's care that she'd allowed herself to be totally exhausted, allowed herself to be taken care of. Janet kept her in bed, permitting Hank only brief visits at mealtime—time for her father to let his pride in her show. She hadn't won the race on the back of a Sinclair Arab, but she was a Sinclair. She saw herself as a Sinclair now, one with her own life to lead, a life that would be mostly apart from the others, but this would be a place to come to be with those she could call family.

"I came here to look at my property," she said. "I've done that. I've found that it isn't really mine, but I'm welcome here. I'll come back often, I think, but I can't just move in here." She gave her head another brave toss. "I have to get on with my own business, don't I?"

"Your business can be here, too."

"Henry's business is here, and Kyle's. Janet is a lovely

woman, and this is her house." Brenna flashed a bright smile. "They're getting married, you know."

"It's about time."

"Yes, it is. She's been very patient."

"So have I," he told her, lifting a hand to tuck her hair behind an ear. The scent of wildflowers reminded him of the view of the meadow from his bedroom window and of the purple flower that had caught Brenna's fancy. He wished they were there now. "I wanted to see you yesterday, but Janet barred the door. I figured you probably had some ideas about leaving."

Not when he was this close. She could smell the soap on his hand as he touched her cheek lightly and then rested it on her shoulder. "I wouldn't have left without saying..."

"Goodbye?"

She nodded.

He shook his head. "No goodbyes, Brenna. You belong here. Maybe not in this house, but in mine. I'm your home, Brenna. I'm where you're comfortable and secure. I love you."

She plumbed the depths of his dark eyes, and her breath was trapped briefly in her throat. "You've never said so."

"Neither have you."

"I was afraid," she told him quietly.

"So was I. I'm a 'common' man, and I guess I thought falling in love with a woman, wanting to give her a home and have a family was probably pretty common behavior."

"Did you think I'd have a problem with that?"

He lifted a shoulder, glancing to the top of her head, where the sunlight from the window caught the red-gold gleam in her hair. "Some women do."

"I'm not like my mother."

"I didn't know your mother. I knew mine. But you're not like her, either. You're not a quitter."

"You wanted me to quit."

"You were tired. You were cold and wet, and I wanted to call a halt to the whole insanity. But you, lady, are no quitter." He noticed the flutter in the breath she drew, and he remembered how fragile she'd looked wrapped in that blanket, and how fierce the look in her eyes had been when she told him she was going to finish the race. She would live up to her commitments.

"What do you need to make you happy, Brenna? Anything you left behind in Connecticut?" She shook her head. He brushed the backs of his fingers under her jaw. "I love you. Just tell me what you need. I'll find a way…"

"Ask me to stay, Cord. Tell me you want me to—"

"Stay," he groaned, pulling her into his arms. "Stay with me and let me love you."

Brenna slid her arms around Cord's neck, buried her face in his hair and whispered, "If you'll let me love you." Then she tilted her head back for his kiss, the one that told her she was something worth keeping.

* * * * *

A marriage of convenience?

SPOUSE FOR HIRE

This January, don't miss our newest three-story collection about three resourceful women who hire husbands for a limited time. But what happens when these three handsome, charming and impossibly sexy husbands turn out to be too good to let get away? Is it time to renegotiate?

THE COWBOY TAKES A WIFE
by *Joan Johnston*

COMPLIMENTS OF THE GROOM
by *Kasey Michaels*

SUTTER'S WIFE
by *Lee Magner*

Available January 1999
wherever Harlequin and Silhouette books are sold.

HARLEQUIN®
Makes any time special ™

Silhouette®

Look us up on-line at: http://www.romance.net   PSBR199

If you enjoyed what you just read,
then we've got an offer you can't resist!

Take 2 bestselling
love stories FREE!

Plus get a FREE surprise gift!

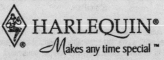

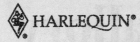